D1477803

MAGIC

MAGIC

Janice Elliott

HODDER AND STOUGHTON
LONDON SYDNEY AUCKLAND TORONTO

British Library Cataloguing in Publication Data
Elliott, Janice
  Magic.
  I. Title
  823'.914[F]   PR6009.L/

  ISBN 0 340 34275 7

Hodder and Stoughton Editorial Office: 47 Bedford Square, London WC1B 3DP.

For Penelope and Robert Steane

PART ONE

PART ONE

1

'*K*ippers!' he said, 'Yes!' and put in his teeth.

When the sun shone into his eyrie, those were the better awakenings. Oliver Hartley could almost, then, have believed in paradise: the molten gold that pierced his curtained eyes spoke of something more than coffin-lids, earth closing, worms. Thus, he felt sure, the light had fallen on his childhood cot and then, as now, he had squeezed his eyes tight shut to keep the gold in and the world out a little longer. The Light of Reason, his father had intoned in his fine voice—sententious old bugger, Bart, parson and goat. Emeritus.

Not much sleep nowadays but small dreams of intense reality, their nature depending upon the blandness or otherwise of his supper. Bread and milk last night so he had been dancing with Kitty—the polka it must have been, for he had woken dizzy, clutching the sides of his bed.

Now, as always upon morning awakening, he checked first that he was alive. A wiggle of the toes confirmed a heart still pumping, but this tingling in the legs, pins and needles as if the circulation had been switched off at night: a damned boiler that might not fire one morning. His age: they all made such a fuss about it. Oliver found it no cause for triumph. When he thought about it he resented it, that was all.

Left arm! Right arm! No stroke in the night, sir. The whinge of rheumatics though and traitorous damp-eyed morning spirit overhears. *I must be gone: there is a grave/ Where daffodil and lily wave*. Mush. Pap. I'd have shown you. Remember, eh, Kitty? The first time you came to the island I waded out and carried you ashore. Lost your shoe, your stockinged feet trailing in the water. You wore something green, seaweed-colour, mermaid wife. Give us back our shouting days.

But you won't, will you, our Father in Heaven, old sod.

He must have spoken aloud, for one of the cats flicked the tip of its tail, jumped off the bed and out through the window onto the conservatory roof. The others, roused, stretched, shuddered, dug their claws into Oliver's lean shanks and complained.

His body reviewed, Oliver blew into the speaking-tube and shouted, not as loudly as he would have liked for fear of his teeth: 'Mrs Humble! Kippers, French toast and Earl Grey!'

Susan Humble brought the water to boil, dropped in the plastic bags of boned kippers, sniffed as she always did, suspiciously, at the packet of Earl Grey and went back to her rose-patterned cup of Indian real English tea. On the way up to the house this morning she had paused in the orchard in the hope of mushrooms and stood, soaking her black laced shoes in the dew, allowing herself for the moment she could spare to perceive the shining webs slung from tree to tree. Poor Susan, Sukie Humble's plain as pie, shall her live or shall her die? But she had stood out the playground chant and she knew beauty when she saw it. Never lie in marriage bed, never courted, never wed. True enough, the first and the last—yet there had been one, a travelling man, gentleman of the road. He'd touched her cheek, and once brought her wild flowers—those field daisies that smell like poison in the house.

Then him up there waiting for his kippers had named her Missis. Courtesy title, he said, and Susan liked that. It sounded like curtsy.

In the orchard she had seen the cat jump from the window—the sign he'd be wanting his breakfast. She sighed and went in.

That evening, exhausted by the journey, the summons, the cigarettes she had smoked without eating, Virginia stood on deck for the twenty-minute crossing. Lights of mainland and island, otherwise utter darkness, lashing rain. She pulled up her collar and turned to face the spray. The sweet, sad voice of the bell-buoy. Die, she used to think it was saying, die. Approached in darkness and wild weather, the island might have been a great ship passing. In some conditions, no more than the stroke of a grey-blue finger on the horizon, yielding herself slowly as the sun burned away the mist, carrying bravely her crazy turrets and spires and flags; and the Hartley house.

Ginny shivered: a madwoman talking to the weather on deck.

Mag, her sister, waiting impatiently in the battered Ford estate—Ginny could imagine her tapping blunt fingernails on the wheel. Peck on the cheek. Mag threw the holdall into the back, slammed the door, drove like a maniac, strong wrists, smoking. She smelled of dog and horse.

'How is father?'

'Up to his old tricks again. You should have rung.'

'The telegram?'

'Sent it himself.'

Virginia slumped. 'My God. Not ill?'

'You mean good or bad not ill?' Mag threw the car round a slippery corner between the island's high hedges. She wound down her window a crack to throw out the cigarette butt and Virginia caught a breath of honeysuckle.

Virginia shook her head. It was nearly funny. What if after Prithee undo this button, old Lear had lived to plague the life out of Cordelia?

They were there. She ran through the rain to the house.

'When will I see Pippa?'

'Tomorrow, if you go over to Fairwater.'

'How is she?'

'Breeding.'

Virginia and Mag were drinking whisky at the kitchen table. Mag shook her head.

'No, I don't mean imminent. It's just that she has so many I assume her to be permanently in pig. I think she does it to keep himself at bay. Well, I'm off. Your bed's made. Good luck.' Mag pushed herself up from the table. Abruptly she hugged her sister, and at that moment the bell rang, relic of days when there was someone, always, to answer. 'Families are hell, aren't they,' said Mag. 'Dogs are best.' And with a slap of her thigh, off she went with her wolf-hound into the wild night.

Virginia knocked, paused and opened the bedroom door. A cat flicked past her ankle. There was a smell of kipper. The window was open and the rain blowing in. She shut it, pulled the curtains, and only then turned to pluck yet another cat from her father's chest—a tabby that scratched. Virginia sucked her thumb and surveyed her father. Oliver's skin was lizard-dry, cobwebbed with time, but his eye, when he shammed waking from sleep, was bright.

'Virginia, Ginny! My wanderer come home!'

She kissed the offered cheek. 'Father—' She meant to reproach.

13

'Forgiven?' His head on one side, posture of a listening bird.

Virginia sighed. 'Why do you do it? Mag and Pippa—'

'Your sisters are boring.'

A thought occurred to her. 'Father, have you by any chance sent anyone else a telegram like mine?'

'One or two.'

'How many?'

'Perhaps three?'

'And there's nothing the matter with you at all.'

'Nothing that death won't cure,' he said cheerfully. A Siamese leaped from the top of the wardrobe, grumbling like a seagull. 'Anyway, I felt like a party. You'll all have one at my funeral. Why shouldn't I be there?'

'Oh God. A wake for the living.' But it was, in its frightful way, a good joke—she saw that.

'You'll stay?'

'Tomorrow, Father. We'll see tomorrow.'

He called after her like a child hoping for a picnic, wheedling, sly: 'We might have another go at Cerdic, eh?'

'You're not still on that?'

'The old Saxon pirate. We'll get him yet. Send down a ferret. Flush him out. You'll see.' He was talking to himself now, his own best audience. Thankfully, Virginia felt herself dismissed.

When Oliver could not sleep, he imagined that he was Britain, lying down. One foot at the Lizard—being,

14

before Land's End, the truly southernmost point of the mainland though not of the realm—the other around the Thames estuary. Right fist flung out to the edge of the bed and clenched for Ulster. There was a rumble, demanding a biscuit, in the Midlands area of his trunk, below the heart, but his head—Scotland, resting on her granite pillow, was weary and refused. Albion slept.

In the hills above Menton, Katherine Hartley, Kitty, Oliver's wife, small, brittle-boned and baked to lizard (*désechée!* they cried at the beauty parlour down that eternally wiggly hill, and held up dried straws of hair but she loved the sun so went no more). Kitty, neither dead nor divorced nor even properly separated, simply distanced, stretched on her warm terrace and pushed the telegram to the far side of her breakfast tray, face down.

There is an island illness, Kitty Hartley told her sleeping cat. Did you know? Even islanders are susceptible, going from England to her smaller islands. No wonder we stole continents. Think of India! To have all that land at one's back: the solace of it. She had remarked once, startling a bridge four, that it can be a shock to inlanders to face the soup from which we made such an arduous evolutionary ascent. There are some ordeals, like childbirth, one prefers to forget.

The Mediterranean, which was no more than a shudder of the light all those precipitous hills below, could be envisaged more comfortably as a pond encircled by warm and powerful land masses. Here, on her perch below the Saracen fort, Kitty could snuff the warm breath of Africa. She rubbed a geranium petal between her fingers and smiled: she had always abhorred sweetness, loved the sharper scents of pelargonia, conifer, chrysanthemum, rosemary, and verbena's green bite.

When Kitty first saw the Hartley house, she laughed. That gay, absurd little island, so jaunty in the sea of small squabbling waves set at odds by wind blowing against tide that made the motor launch bounce. Then her best green frock was splashed, stepping ashore, so she jumped into Oliver's arms.

And then, oh my dear, the house, Kitty would say, you should have seen it! English rectory with Turkish minarets and Spanish palms.

(Walking in the shade in the market, in the street, the old woman, the eccentric Englishwoman, spoke audibly, smiling as at a tea party, sometimes laughing aloud or scowling at her invisible company, whacking a stone with her stick. She did no harm.)

What looked like a fig leaf on the flagstone by Kitty's chair was a tiny salamander. I am like that, she thought, transfixed on my warm rock. And now comes this summons to wrench me away. She crumpled the telegram into a ball and threw it at the sleeping cat who woke, complained and would not play. Sour puss. To go or not to go? Another of Olly's tricks? Kitty dozed, as she often did nowadays: a sleep that did not refresh but alarmed her—one day, she thought, I'll catnap my way into eternity. Oblivion, rather. Apart from a small door she kept ajar to the possibility of reincarnation, Kitty believed—for herself at least—in extinction. Olly, she considered, had invented God to shout at, storming up Poet's Walk to Cerdic's throne above the lighthouse to wave his fist at an empty sky. When they were young, they had made love there on the same spot. A hiker had caught them and they hadn't cared.

'Sometimes,' she had told her grandson, Sandy, when he brought his girl here in the spring, 'when I first knew it, the island seemed enchanted. Douce, you know—soft. All honeysuckle, sunsets and dog roses. Even the cattle had the softest eyes I've ever seen. But then there was rapture—your grandfather was so persuasive he could impose his vision. Well, I daresay he still can.'

Sandy had stretched his long legs. The girl he had brought from Rome—Flora? Dora?—sat very still. She wore a neat, grave smile. She never fiddled with her thick chestnut hair, and hardly spoke. At night Kitty heard them making love and then the girl did give voice: a mew like a seagull.

Sandy said, 'When I was small I thought he owned the island.' He smiled. He had suddenly, this year, gone from elbowed gawky awkwardness to something like beauty. He was supposed to be a problem, Virginia's

17

son, but his grandmother—not the doting type—saw him as a dreamer, gentle, one who gave pleasure. Sandy turned to include his girl. 'In some weather you can't see it from the mainland. It disappears. The first time I saw that my mother said look, it's vanished, and I screamed my head off.' The girl opened her eyes wider but did not stir. Kitty examined her for flaws and detected bitten finger-nails. She felt more kindly disposed towards her.

'I should keep away from the island,' she said. 'I daresay it's pretty still, but not what it was. And it's too sleepy. Like going to sleep.'

A motor-bike screamed on the Corniche below and Kitty jumped. She had spoken aloud, she realised, and for a moment it seemed that the boy and the girl were still in the garden and even when she had come to her senses Sandy lingered, his presence. When he was small, Kitty had shared dreams with her grandson: that was their secret from Oliver. Unless he shared them too—not uncommon in families—and said nothing, to tease. That would be like him, to plague the household with his dreams; grinning bonily in his bed while he dispatched his phantasms around the night house, scampering, scratching at doors, nuzzling at pillows, laying his cuckoo's eggs in our soft defenceless brains.

Sometimes I think he's dreamed us all, invented us. Or we him.

Wake up, Kitty. You will forget the telegram. You are alone. You will break up your solitude into small parcels. Take your stick. Go to the market, walk in the shade.

Mineral water and salad for lunch. Nap this afternoon, but not too long.

The girl stood by the window in the drab blue light of dawn, shoulders hunched, thin arms across her breast— her way of sulking.

'Will you go?'

Sandy closed his eyes again. The little room gave onto a well of a yard which seemed to contain all the screeching children and barking dogs of Rome.

'Not sure.'

'Are you fond of your grandfather? I liked her, but you never talk about him.'

'Perhaps that's why. Because of her.'

'They fought?'

'Not exactly. Not that I ever heard.' Sandy opened his eyes and considered the ceiling. 'But you couldn't be on both sides: that was understood. And he was stronger. When I was young I thought he was very powerful— that he knew everything, could do anything. Now, I don't know. I can't imagine him dying.'

'I don't want you to go. If you do can I come with you?'

'Grandmother warned you against it.'

'I'd manage.' She came to sit on the edge of the bed. Sandy rubbed his eyes and finally made the tremendous effort of waking, taking in the day.

'Funny. I dreamed of it last night. The island. It's not all the way Grandma describes it, you know. Quite wild in places. I tried to steal gulls' eggs. People jump off the cliffs. Or fall. I used to dare myself: six steps to the edge with my eyes shut.'

The girl could imagine he did. She watched him. He had forgotten her; when he spoke of the island, his eyes were pale, opaque as those of a somnambulist, whose gaze is turned inward and whose dream it is dangerous to break.

2

*O*liver woke at four with a cat on his face. He flung it off, peed in the chamber-pot and, back in bed, dozed fitfully until six, when he reached into the bedside cabinet for the bottle of Milpar that contained something a little stronger.

He had heard the rain last night and hoped for a gale—in a south-westerly the house sailed and he with it, roaring, creaking, old bones, old wood.

But we still have good passages, in time and space.

Alert now, after his little nip, Oliver sat up, pulled an old woollen jacket around him, put on his spectacles and, knocking several books from the dusty pile on the floor, brought aboard *The Voyage of the Beagle*.

Served there, as a midshipman, all five years. Humble knows. Don't tell the others, they'll put you away; my foul nest of daughters. Oliver laid a finger to the side of his nose, grinned, and returned to Patagonia.

Whom may a man detest but his own daughters?

He shifted in the bed. Old age is not wisdom but piles. Too much sitting, writing, reading, when he should have been striding the bridge, stretching his legs. Yet there was a time when he could outstride them all; in late afternoon, standing at the top of the cliff walk above the lighthouse, the sun behind him, he cast a long shadow and the others with their picnic-baskets and scarfs and walking sticks and rugs and wraps, ran around in his darkness. Then Oliver would lower himself to sit, resting on one elbow on the dry, wind-blown grass; so they would be in the sun again, he had given it to them, they would continue their scramble up the hill.

'Oof!' Kitty had gasped, 'it's too much. Too much for me today.'

As it turned out, Kitty, four months married, was pregnant.

Oliver had put his ear to Kitty's belly.

'It tickles. It's nice,' she had said. 'What are you doing?' She wound her fingers in his wiry hair to hold him there; she would have drawn him in, if she could. He gave her such wild feelings. She might have contained the world, she was boundless.

'Listening to my son.'

'How do you know it's a boy?' This time she tugged his hair, quite hard.

'But of course it's a boy. It must be.' Oliver looked up, startled.

Kitty thought: that's what redeems his arrogance—his innocence. The assumption that the world will always tick his way. She smiled. In spite of her own strong nature, she was at that time still pottily in love with this angular young husband; jagged not only in

22

body but mind. 'He could do with the edges taken off him,' her own father had remarked mildly, looking up from his book. He kept his finger between the pages. If someone had asked him one minute later what he had said, he would have forgotten he had spoken at all.

'Well, it kicks like a soldier,' Kitty had said, 'so I daresay you're right.'

The book slipped from Oliver's hand. He breathed with a rattling snore, mouth open. In a dream of childhood he lay on his stomach at the edge of the lawn in the spiky grass and observed his sainted father, Bible in hand, stalk the new maid, their figures wading deeply through the shaking air. Then, in nightmare, the giant father spied Oliver and turned with a soundless roar.

'Dreaming,' said Mrs Humble, rattling back the curtains. 'That would be cheese last night.' 'Old fool,' she meant, and he knew. They could speak without words, almost, in silent accord or dumb quarrel. 'You'll be getting up, with her here.' Humble made this a statement as she set down his cup.

Oliver pulled the eiderdown up to his nose. 'I was dreaming of your mother.'

'I daresay.' She would not be coaxed. Implacable Humble.

Oliver sniffed. 'I shan't get up again. I shall write no more.'

'Oh, yes.' Humble turned to survey him; her spectacles were opaque, unreadable, she was often passed over for her blankness, it made her invisible—and yet there were things she saw and understood, visions even. She knew she would be mocked for them and kept to herself: silly Sukie saw an angel in the cabbage patch, came on the devil netted in a thorn bush, heard the bells beneath the sea and the voices of dead sailors in the wind. Only Oliver knew this. She let him write it, but not in her name. And he told her he had been in this world before and would be again, though never in the same shape. A seaman, he said he had been, and a god and a beetle and some he could not remember. A beetle—that made Sukie Humble laugh. Better than Bingo, she told her canary. He'll be a budgie next time, maybe. Too much reading, she reckoned, and that stuff he wrote. She liked television herself. You could receive it. It entered into you just as they said the Holy Ghost might come. She'd walk round with last night's telly in her head, something to think about all day. She'd knitted a Fair Isle sweater for Richard Baker and he signed a letter to say thank you, but never wore it. Humble didn't mind.

There wasn't much she did mind, now she came to think about it. Only when the map of her days was disturbed Humble was bothered. She was bothered now.

'Well, do as you like, but there's only eggs. Poached, scrambled or boiled?'

'Fried.'

'Poached then, with a nice bit of toast.'

*

24

Virginia wondered why she felt nervous of telephoning her husband from her father's house. It was absurd, childish.

'Sam?' She looked round to make sure she'd closed the study door. It was a bad line. 'Sorry to ring so early.' Sam would be in the bright morning kitchen, yawning over black coffee and trying to get Lucy off to school. Thinking of them both, there, in the house, Virginia shivered; her arms felt empty. The study had always been cold and dark, the place where Grandfather made his sermons.

'When are you coming back?'

'I don't know. Has Lucy gone to school?'

'I can't find a clean shirt.'

'Don't forget her dinner money.'

'How is he?'

Virgina shifted. This had been the room of childhood nightmare, by day a door to run past. She remembered her grandfather had long, thin fingers he could crack. He put butterflies in a killing jar and fixed them under glass.

'Oh, false alarm.'

'You can come back then?'

'Well, I'm not sure.'

'Look, I must go. What are you not sure of?'

'I don't know. I'm sorry, I really don't know.'

Unlike Virginia and Sandy, Sam had never cared for the island. A mainland man, he was bewildered by her passion for it, how it drew her.

'Call me again, then.'

Virginia laid back the receiver gently in its cradle. She went from the study to the dim hall, where she stood, looking up the stairs to the door of her father's room. She shivered. She thought Mag might be wrong: he could be dying. She did not know what she felt about this. It would be the abrupt silencing of a force of nature with which she had frequently contended and she could not imagine what they would be left with—peace or a void.

'As far as I'm concerned,' said Mag, 'the old sod can rot. You let him use you, Ginny.' She had arrived with a box of groceries and was off again. 'He tried it with Pippa and me. Mostly me, as I wasn't supposed to have responsibilities—just kennels to run. He'd yell for help and shout at us when we got here. Get back to London. Leave him to Humble—she likes it.'

Virginia mused. 'I'm worried about the house. The roof's in a bad state and every room downstairs is damp. There's a crack in the dining-room.'

Mag was cheerful. 'Falling down, of course. About time too.'

They were standing at the door. Virginia looked up at the house, rosy in the autumn light. 'That would be sad.'

'You're too soft. You always were. Daddy's girl.'

Soft, thought Virginia, as she turned away, across the lawn past neglected beds of leggy Michaelmas daisies and last year's chrysanthemums, towards the once-revolving summerhouse where she and Pippa had played home and later read the *Karma Sutra* and hated Mag—softness does not come into it. My nerves are tangled with this place—the house, the island—it is my history, it poaches on the present and the future. I think sometimes it will not let me live.

In 1937, Mag, Kitty's first child, took three days to be born and came in on a gale.

Oliver, who could never stay still, stood for three days outside Kitty's bedroom, scowling at those who went in to attend the labour, accosting those who came out. He ate hard-boiled eggs and dozed on his feet, like the long-legged bird he resembled.

'Can I get you some toast, Sir Oliver?' the housemaid, Humble's mother, had said (getting on for a maid, she panted from the stairs or from the rector's attentions—he still pinched her bottom). Her daughter, Susan—an unnoticeable child—was playing with a potato doll in the kitchen. It was the shape of a baby. She wrapped it in a dishcloth and talked to it strictly.

'Or a chair?'

Oliver had looked wildly at the housemaid, as if accosted by a madwoman railing.

The casements rattled, spume broke on the pier, smaller seabirds were tossed ashore, wind tore at the racing clouds and Mag was delivered—an eight-and-a-half-pound breech birth.

At the news that he was the father of a healthy girl, Oliver sat down for the first time in three days and burst into tears. The midwife was touched by such a display of emotion. The doctor grunted.

'After your Aunt Margaret's birth,' Kitty once told her grandson, Sandy, 'I would have moved back to the mainland. The rectory no longer seemed so amusing, and it was difficult with your great-grandfather.'

Sandy grinned. 'Chasing maids?'

Kitty sipped her lemon juice and soda through a straw, frowning slightly at something she did not wish to recollect.

'Well, that. And, of course, your grandfather and your great-grandfather . . . they didn't get on, you know. It was war in heaven, with Oliver the rebel angel because he wouldn't go into the Church. Oh dear! What a fuss. And then Alice's death. I'll be boring you. Young people don't want to hear about those silly old things. It was a pity though. If I'd had a son. Oliver was frightfully upset that Margaret was a girl, he cried his eyes out, the nurse thought how lucky I was to have such a loving husband! Well, he did love me, we were still in love. But then there were two more girls. Poor Olly. Life's a muddly thing, isn't it?'

'Poor Gran.'

'No. Not at all. Really, I have been a fortunate woman.' She patted his hand briskly. 'I am fortunate now, with you here.'

*

In the thirties, when the Spitview Hotel was opened, Kitty, the baby and the nurse, found themselves sharing the beach of pure pale sand with nannies, children and mothers of the better families. The island had always been a popular alternative to Frinton but the Spitview doubled its appeal. Beside the newcomers, many of those who had previously taken a house were drawn by the attractions offered by the new hotel: an early nursery high tea for the children and nannies, dinner-dances later for the adults—the pleasures of society to relieve the obligation of a family holiday. Those who would meet at other times of year in Scotland, London, or at Deauville, Biarritz, Cap Martin, would encounter the same crowd here, playing bridge, playing golf, dancing, flirting over cocktails in the Captain's Cabin or the new American Bar preferred by the women. And the air was so delicious! A heady mingling of ozone, honeysuckle, myrtle and unseen herbs. Couples in evening dress sipped it as they strolled on the beach beyond the loom of light and music, the women swaying against the men—limp tulips on their silly heels. They drifted and called to one another among the dunes, esparto grass, sea lavender and wild lupins. At the high-water mark, the sensible turned back, the carefree slipped off their sandals and walked on, the wicked whispered and laughed and shed their silk stockings to run barefoot on the cool wet sand; when the tide came in and ebbed again it scoured the beach clean of their dancing prints.

There was—still is—a dangerous current in the entrance channel at certain states of tide. A child was drowned there one sunny August afternoon when the beach was crowded: his cry was lost among the shouts of playing children. His nurse had fallen asleep over her knitting.

Another time, a young woman—one of the dancers—for a dare, or because she was a little drunk, kicked off her sandals and jumped in. She was a strong swimmer but could not breast the ebb. It is surprising there were not more fatalities. Soon after this a warning notice was put up and a lifebuoy.

'Where was I?' said Kitty. 'Oh yes. Your grandfather and I were very naughty—that was another reason, of course, for the quarrels with his father—we went to the Spitview Hotel to dance! From the rectory! But we did love to dance. And, you see, the Hartleys were not your poor church-mice. Not rich, but Oliver's mother's family took shares in the railways at the right time and she left a nice cut of the cake to Oliver. They were an old island family. It was quite famous for its railway.

'Everyone nowadays thinks we were all depressed in the thirties. That's History for you, lumping us all in the same boat. But it wasn't bad for us. We had fun.

'When I remember the dancing, I can forget the rest. The bad part. It is human to remember but sometimes I think one should practise forgetfulness. Yes, that would be best.'

Remember! Let go of nothing, Oliver believed. Every scrap of the past he wanted to snatch back and lock up in his head. He hoarded old letters and diaries, wrote on any scrap of paper that came to hand, to friends, acquaintances, some he had never met, many dead, demanding peremptorily names, dates, facts, gossip, the grand and the trivial, the bright rags and banners of a long life. Some were even posted. (Some Virginia found in a tea caddy; she put them back and felt the uncomfortable wrench of tearless pity.)

To Ralph Stephens, a contemporary at Oxford and colleague in the Foreign Office: 'Remind me exact date Hindenburg's funeral. We left Berlin in time for old Joffre buried Paris. Funeral year, eh? Remember that damnfool helmet? . . .' *To local archivist*: 'Madam—my *intensive* researches for proposed history of island reveal serious discrepancies in your evidence for dating of Roman pavement at Rading . . .' Many to his wife. Were they ever posted? Only Kitty knew and Humble perhaps. 'My darling little Kitty, I am out of sorts and crabby without you, a nuisance all round . . . How can I ever finish my History in this disordered house? The food they give me! Humble's slops of mince and cabbage, bread and milk, fit for hens.' 'Kitty! Why do you not answer? I would atone . . .' Another time to Virginia: 'Your mother is an obstinate old woman who prefers exile to her own roof. I have attempted to reason with her *time and again* but I believe it must be senile dementia that sets her against her family. If I knew of what misdeed I stand accused . . .'

On the back of a bill (unpaid): 'What will become of this History I cannot imagine. I am in a mumble of myth. I dream of this kingdom and her lost islands, drowned cities: Lyonesse, Cantref, old Scilly, St Michael's, the people under the sea.'

This scrap was in the deed box of notes he gave Virginia to sort. She paused over it, caught by the image of figures moving heavily through water, arms outstretched, like blind men, not touching. People. Families. She was sitting in the window-seat with its view over trees to the sea. She turned to Oliver. It occurred to her that he had no intention of finishing his History, because once it was concluded he would have no reason to live.

Was he dozing or shamming? His head was turned to one side on the pillow, his eyes were shut, but his mouth was closed, no snore. So exhaustingly alive awake, like this he appeared in metamorphosis, his cobwebbed features halfway to dust.

'Father?' Virginia spoke softly. He muttered and twitched his head from side to side on the pillow; the grip of his hands on the sheet tightened, then his eyes opened. He did not recognise her at once and she wondered from what dream she had snatched him.

'Father, you must get up. Have your tea and get up.'

'I told Humble, I'm staying here. What have I to get up for?'

Virginia sighed, refusing to be trapped.

'It's bad for you. Bad for your lungs. You'll get sores. You need a bath.'

'Who cares what is bad for me?' He sulked. She was exasperated. The old pattern.

'We all do.'

Oliver snorted. 'I'm changing my will, you know.' The thought seemed to invigorate him. 'Not a bite of the old man for those two bitches.' He grinned wickedly, sparked by malice. What he wanted was a fight, a showdown from which he would withdraw one moment before it was too late. Virginia knew the game and had played it, but not today, she had no heart for it today.

'Do you want to work any more?'

He knew when to give in. He shook his head. 'Time for *Blue Peter*. Well, turn it on, woman.'

'Lucy watches that.'

Virginia fetched the tea. She did not draw the curtains. They sat before the television, a crackle of brightness. The light ebbed from the room.

3

Well, I will have my say, since I—Susan Humble—
was there and saw most of it; and what I didn't see
my mother told me or I guessed. Not that I gossip. Not
that I haven't other things to think of besides the
Hartley family. I'll see the old man off and then I might
do some travelling round the world a bit—I could
surprise them all.

They don't notice Susan Humble much. That's how I
know, whether I want to or not, like a mirror.

When Margaret was born I got a potato in the shape
of a baby and wrapped it in a dishcloth—the sort they
used to crochet in string—and pretended it was the one
upstairs. I told it what to do. That's what children need,
I say. I played with it for two days until it was naughty
and I put it in the pan. When I see Margaret sometimes I
think of her boiling away and it gives me a laugh. If my
mother had known she'd have walloped me, if she'd
noticed—she had enough on her hands with the old
reverend.

*

'Father and Mother,' Virginia said, 'they seem like people I've heard of in a story. Do you know what I mean?' She raised her face to the light, her eyes closed. As she walked over to Fairwater, to Pippa's, the sun had come out, dazzling her. This southern back of the island was famous for sun. Drunken wasps sipped at the golden apples in Pippa's orchard on the slope where geese grazed and Bramley, Worcester and Cox's embraced unpicked. Plenitude and excess. Beauty and muddle. Pippa. Virginia raised her hand to shade her eyes. Yes, Mag might be right—Pippa did look pregnant again. Not so much her figure, swamped in any case under sweaters and smock, but something about the eyes, a slow, already sway-backed way of walking.

Pippa shifted an infant from one knee to the other to reach for her mug of coffee. She pondered. Virginia saw her like that: a soft child who, in thought, bit her lip as she did now. The one with the beautiful smile who cried easily, silent tears running like oil down her cheeks. Mag used to bully her, pulling her thick, pale plaits, hiding her dolls. Grown, Pippa had married Eric—apple-man to her pear-woman—and learned to put on vagueness; or her children had blurred both her features and her capacity for pain. She nodded.

'Mr and Mrs Lear. Shakespeare never says what she was like, does he?'

'Can't remember. Much the same as Mother, I should think. Not that I've seen Mother lately. Sandy does.' Virginia was by no means certain that she wanted to talk about Sandy, even to Pippa.

Her son had her sisters' fair colouring. In company with any of them Virginia felt sharp, dark, skinny—a Celt among Saxons, Father said. Perhaps that was why she had been attracted to her husband, Sam Conti? Celt rejoining her tribe. Thinking of Sam, she smiled.

'How's Eric?' Virginia need hardly have asked: Eric was always well, it was impossible to imagine Eric, with his pink cheeks and clean hands, anything but well.

House market down, Pippa was saying, the recession, autumn, you know; but he was learning to play the church organ. He already sang in the choir: a lapse for which Oliver had excommunicated him long ago. Pippa dipped her head. Regarding Virginia from behind her child's curls, she coloured.

'I'm just sorry there's that thing with him and Father. It makes it difficult. And then everything falls on you. I feel bad.'

'Oh well.' Virginia leaned back in the deckchair, hand brushing the grass. In the shelter of the wall it was still warm, there was heat enough to tug scents from the earth. The island awaited the first frost long after mainland gardens had been nipped. She had forgotten.

She was almost asleep when Pippa spoke.

'How is Sandy?'

'In London or it might be Rome with someone called Flora. Or it might be Dora. Yes, Dora. When last heard of. Ask Mother.'

Pippa always flushed for anyone else's discomfiture. If you trod on her foot she apologised.

'Sorry. Well.'

36

Virginia shrugged. 'What worries me is I can't think what he lives on. Dora perhaps? Hope so. Dora—isn't that a weird name when you think about it? Never hear it nowadays.' She opened her mouth to continue but changed her mind. Since childhood she had never got over the habit of protecting Pippa—then, from Mag, stray dogs, school bullies, Father's sardonic tongue; now from her own problems. It seemed miscasting that not gentle Pippa, but she, should be Father's favourite. She stood, pulling on her jacket.

'I must be gone. The King calls.' The sisters walked slowly to the gate. In the mixed hedge honeysuckle made a small, late flowering. Pippa snapped off a dead rose-head, gone to seed.

'How's Humble?'

Virginia laughed. 'Battier than ever. She really is out of *Cold Comfort Farm*. Or perhaps it's just those spectacles. I think the two of them are up to something, though I can't imagine what.'

The sisters embraced, then Pippa said, 'I'll walk down the lane with you.' She hoisted the baby onto her hip, called to the others to stay in the garden. The latest was a boy, already twisting strongly to escape from his mother's arms. Virginia thought, you let them go, you have to let them go, you're proud that it doesn't hurt; then suddenly your arms feel empty.

Pippa was saying, 'It sounds silly, but I've always had the feeling that Father was keeping a secret. Not necessarily bad or good, just something we weren't to be told. D'you know what I mean?'

37

Virginia nodded. 'I hadn't thought of it but now you say so, I wouldn't be surprised. I daresay Humble knows.'

Pippa grinned. 'Humble knows everything. D'you remember that story? Hans Andersen or was it Grimm? About Mother Elder who was Memory? I was reading it to the children the other day and we had it when we were small. Well, that's Humble! And you know what happened to her in the end? They put her in the teapot!'

The sisters began to laugh, giggling like girls, affronting the baby, laughing till they cried. By the time they had sobered they had reached the end of the lane.

It turned colder as Virginia walked up the hill and across the downs, through the wood and past the abbey where, as a child, she had screamed at the glimpse of a monk hurrying, hooded and head bowed, in the twilight among the mothy bats. By the time she got back it was dark.

He was neglected. His own daughter came to see him—was *sent for*—and spent half her time running around the island. The other three had not even answered the telegrams—if Humble had sent them.

Oliver reached for the speaking-tube, then remembered that Humble would have gone home early, with Ginny here. He was confused. He clung like a child to routine and once it was broken in the smallest way, a crack appeared in the fabric of his life through which chaos might enter, birds peck his marrow, leaves dance in his skull.

It was the other way round when he was young and the *agent provocateur*. What his father called the dubious privilege of a private income was to play merry hell. The money was on Mama's side and she left it all to me, to spite him—revenge for those thousand years of cold church and hot housemaids.

This quilt is frayed. If one could take a thread, twitch, tug, and draw it through the fabric of one's life to trace its path and beginning . . . events most distanced from one another might be seen as connected. Even explained? (In spite of the fact that the study of history reveals behind most cataclysms an excuse, an irresistible movement constituted of the most disparate particles— never an explanation. If explanations were the key, then Marx would have had his English revolution. Still one tries. Accident is repugnant to the historian, don't you think? Oh, you are not there. No one is there. They have left me in the dark.)

A pretty silver thread here, though the overall effect is plum, plain as a plum; a little closer and there's a peacock sheen. Finally, as on approaching earth from space, one loses the patchwork and is devoured by detail. If I were to pull this thread . . .

Humble and Ginny had conspired to put out the cats. Alcestis mewed in silent reproach at the window. The conservatory roof, where she complained with waving tail, was lit by the porch-lamp so that she appeared haloed by light. Oliver cocked his head and, hearing no sound below, put his feet cautiously to the ground, nipped across to the window and let in his love. Only when he was back in bed did he wonder how he was to explain with what feline ingenuity Alcestis had shut the window behind her, assuming it to be unlatched in the first place.

Through his cardigan and pyjama top Alcestis raked Oliver's thin chest painfully. Such passion! Why do I tolerate it? Nowadays I accept even a semblance of love wherever I might find it.

Too much. He took her by the scruff and flung her off the bed. She twitched her tail and swore at him. He grinned.

The front door slammed, Ginny coming in. The house shook. Oliver curled into a foetal position, the quilt up to his nose. Winter was coming, the wind getting up. Our house is falling. The roof will fly off, the windows implode. Our enemies gather and threaten. If I squeeze my eyes tight I can see it: Cerdic's castle crumbles, the sea reclaims the piers, the flowers and downs are drowned and I with them, old Cronus.

Bar the doors, stuff the keyholes, man the attics!

Humble cooked herself a frozen chicken pancake. It was a blessing what they could do nowadays, although she did not accept science wholemeal. Not those unnatural spare parts, never knowing whose kidney you were wearing. They were nice young people on *Tomorrow's World* but she never watched hospital programmes. What about the soul? she always thought.

She tipped the pancake onto her plate, put the plate on a tray with napkin, knife and fork, and carried her tea into the little front parlour her mother had never used, even though it got the evening sun. After supper she would let the canary out to fly around the room, such a pretty, darting, twittering yellow even if he couldn't talk.

On *South Today* they said someone on the island was building lifesize fibreglass dinosaurs for trippers. Fancy that.

In St Marie-la-Douce Kitty ate her omelette by the open window. By now most of the tourists had left and the few resident expatriates emerged from their little gardens or shaded balconies to enjoy the still-warm air. Through the winter, for those with a taste for blood, there would be violent bridge, but meanwhile they perambulated their stiff bones for a last baking, stretched their arthritic claws in greeting—crab hailing crab. The brigadier raised his stick, Kitty nodded down and enjoyed an absurd impulse to toss him a scarlet geranium head, imagined him catching it in his teeth to a trumpet's flourish.

She sipped her wine. Although she took care to measure her days into portions, made the omelette *fines herbes* just so, powdered the dry flesh that might

41

be better oiled, marched the protesting limbs for a promenade, sent for a new biography, wrote a letter and hoped for one, took up painting and gave up a gin, Kitty found she had very little present. Time was not now.

Kitty spoke aloud to immanent presences who took their seats upon her balcony:

The Mistral is on the way: my rheumatics tell me. Do you find any relief in those copper bracelets?

Oh look! There is the girl from the craft shop wheeling her baby. She is Swedish and speaks English and French to it. No one knows who the father is. I don't believe she knows herself nor does she seem to care. She has the air of a striding madonna, to whom the annunciation came as no surprise.

I am tired. Soon I shall have a little cat-nap, like puss.

Below Kitty's balcony the cicadas still celebrated a summer that was over. As the dusk hesitated there was the Swedish girl wheeling her little boy home. She bent to speak to him and he waved, thrusting his small arms in salute to the old Englishwoman on her balcony where she sat to get the last of the light.

Bonsoir, *mon petit*. *Bonne nuit*. Goodnight.

4

Dora unpacked the shopping: frozen chips, cooking oil, beefburgers with onion, a small bag of brown rice, a carton of milk, joss sticks, a tin of spaghetti, a pack of old-fashioned sanitary towels and various smaller items: garlic, various spices and curry powder. She was wearing a trailing purple skirt, a loose sequinned blouse and a silk shawl. She clanged with bangles.

'The turmeric was too expensive but curry powder's just the same. There wasn't enough for Chinese—we'd better register for benefit tomorrow, if we'll be here long enough.'

Sandy inspected the shopping and groaned.

'Isn't real spaghetti cheaper?'

'Not any more.'

Dora arranged her shopping neatly in the grimy cupboard, shut the door, took a joss stick, lit it and stood it in a jam jar. She smiled and sat down, a bizarre house-wife. This room was, for the moment, her home.

Kitty's grandson, Sandy, and Dora, his girl, had come straight from the boat train to Balham. Since the last riots more shops had been boarded up and to a stranger, on that wet autumn evening, these trailing suburbs would have appeared as merry as the marshes of Hell; but the villagers of London scuttled unamazed to their burrows. So, even after an absence, Sandy and Dora drew the atmosphere of damp decay around them like a shawl, found, vaguely, the comfort of familiarity even in the seediness of the place. Since they were last here more Edwardian dolls' houses had fallen to the middle classes but the black families Sandy and Dora encountered appeared surprisingly unresentful of the stripped-pine invasion. The couple who lived below them, Gloria and Gregory, were pleased to see the Habitat van draw up next door—it gave tone to the street. Nig-nog snobs, Sandy called them to their faces, but they just grinned. After all, as Dora pointed out, it wasn't the television producer down the street who was exploiting them, but the absentee landlord: the Pakistani who ran the sex shop in the High Street—and he, in turn, had his masters. Christopher, the friend who on occasion lent Sandy this room, had once tried to trace them and come up against a Birmingham launderette chain. At that point he had been warned off, and took the advice.

Sandy unrolled his sleeping-bag and lay back on the iron bedstead. He thought one day he might like to do a book on the vanished villages of London. Not quite vanished, rather, for you could still glimpse them, through Balham, Brixton, Wandsworth, endless Streatham: the villas, pubs and churches on a main road that had once been a quiet thoroughfare. The green the city had eaten. His grandmother had been born in Bromley—she pronounced it 'Brummley' quite without affectation—and spoke of it still as country. 'I suppose it was a grand house,' Kitty said, 'though one never thought of that at the time. They said that from it the builders could see the Fire of London.' England, thought Sandy, land of lost hopes and no glory at all, thank God. And yet he was curious about it. Curious and concerned as a distant relative might be attending a deathbed. He loved Kitty's stories.

Then at other times, Sandy wanted no stories, no history. England choked him and he would be off. Abruptly, he felt that now. Yet having just arrived, how could he be off? A beer might help if he could afford it, but Dora was dishing up the rice, onion and curry powder. For someone so fastidious she was a messy cook. She prepared food with the air of a princess who has wandered into the kitchen to play.

'Do we always have to eat that?'

'Until one of us gets a job.' Dora was enragingly reasonable.

The power was off, of course: Christopher hadn't paid the bill. At least, he'd shown them the trick with the gas meter, so they could have a hot meal. Dora lit a candle, transforming the attic room to a cave. She spread a miraculously clean drying-up cloth on the tea chest that served as a table and laid two forks: just so.

'I can't think what we'll do with the frozen stuff. Perhaps Gloria would put it in her fridge.'

'Not sure I feel up to Gloria tonight.'

Dora smiled. She knew what he meant. Her long fingers handling the fork looked frail as twigs, her wrists were thin enough for the child's bracelets he'd bought her in Rome, and her features were sharp with weariness from the journey. She appeared so frangible that even Sandy, knowing better, was touched and drawn to her—just as he had been the first time he saw her, at a Modigliani exhibition. He had come in out of the rain and there she was, the artist's model and mistress, Jeanne Hébuterne, in a shapeless knitted cardigan down to her knees and the kind of rain-hat with elastic under the chin that schoolgirls used to wear. Sandy looked at the painting and looked at the girl.

Dora said, 'She wasn't a bit like that in the photographs. Quite fat, actually, with pudgy hands.'

Sandy smiled. They moved on to another portrait. Sandy glanced over Dora's shoulder at her catalogue. *The Young Swedish Girl (Portrait of Jeanne Hébuterne.)* Here was the rain-hat or something very like it.

Dora always studied paintings with the expression, solemn and politely searching, with which she greeted strangers—or repelled them.

Sandy said, 'Perhaps it was like El Greco? Didn't he have something wrong with his eyes? So he attenuated everything?'

Now it was his turn for the gaze. 'Yes, I believe it was the same. Has it stopped raining?'

They walked out onto the Embankment. She seemed not to mind that he kept her company. The Thames shone, bland and flat. Sandy wondered if the elastic under her chin hurt, and if she would take off her hat.

'Andrew Conti,' he said. 'Sandy.'

'Dora.'

She turned and shook his hand with odd formality, and in the same gesture, at last, pulled off her hat. Her hair tumbled out: long and thick, a little dry, chestnut not red like the girl's in the painting. Sometimes she would take enough to make two plump braids in front which she then twisted to hold back the rest. Less often, she shaped it into a vaguely Egyptian shape, conical and piled very high.

'You look like her,' Sandy said.

'She has a python's neck.' They had reached the outskirts of Pimlico. Dora's mouth curved a little at each corner: it was always hard to tell if she was smiling.

'Do snakes have necks?' She shrugged, definitely a small smile this time. He was reluctant to lose her but, on the other hand, he had no idea where she was heading.

'Are you an art student? I liked the Modiglianis. D'you know about him?'

She paused, bit her lip in study, as though he had asked her a street direction.

'He wrote that fertile laziness is the only real work.'

Sandy nodded, then grinned broadly and kicked a stone into a puddle, scattering some grubby sparrows. Pigeons mated in a window box. The river stared at the dashing sky and was ruffled. Christ, London was beautiful. 'A great man. A truly great man!'

Once, while she slept, Sandy flicked open a notebook she had left. In her neat, small-lettered italic, Dora had written: 'Modigliani's friends tried to take a death-mask but only tore his skin and his hair. He asked Jeanne to follow him to Paradise, although she was nine months pregnant. At dawn she threw herself from the window.'

This night of arrival in England they made love to the jungle drums of Gloria's household, below: a television comedy series at full blast, yelling children, banging doors, barking dogs. On Saturday nights it would be reggae; and sometimes, if the air were still and all the windows open there might be added the ululation of Gloria's orgasms. How she achieved such triumphant satisfactions upon puny little Gregory was a wonder and source of speculation. 'Well, it's technique not size, I suppose,' Dora said, and, if she were wistful, did not show it. Come to think of it, Sandy reflected, there was very little that Dora did show. And yet even saying nothing, at her mousiest, in that awful grey cardigan, she affected people. He was worried about taking her to the island because he felt, protectively, that she might be bothered or bored. On the other hand, might it be she who bothered them?

He drew back then plunged. Dora uttered her seagull mew.

Sandy wondered what it was to feel very deeply, if the English knew how. Perhaps it was there but the climate held it down. Even their crimes were somehow drab. When he was ten or so, his mother caught him pinching his arms. He said it was to try to get warm; it was really to find out how hard he had to pinch before he felt pain. He was disappointed that he could not make himself cry.

In the night the wind got up. They were cold and clung together, both zipped in Sandy's sleeping-bag. He dreamed that he was sailing in a gale with his grand-father, Oliver, roaring at the helm, oilskins soaked, the sea breaking over them, they would be swamped in the deadly curl of green sea. An ambulance ripped the night. Then Sandy and Dora were floating gently, warmly, in each other's arms. They opened their eyes. Gloria had come into the attic room and thrown over them a blanket made of many scraps of coloured wool.

They sat in Gloria's kitchen—or the room, rather, in which Gloria and Gregory had their stove, bed, table, sink, television and refrigerator. The children—ranging from the baby named Fanta (in honour of the American television series) to seventeen-year-old Derek, who called himself Mohammed—slept in the smaller front room.

Sandy told Gloria that they were back from Rome. The rain had stopped and as they drank coffee looking out over the sunny garden in which bloomed broken prams, plant pots, bicycles and a rather beautiful weed, a bird sang. Gloria sighed and hummed, stroking her lap.

'Oh, you poor white folk and your unemployment!' She rolled her eyes and rocked. 'What you pore trash to do? Lordy, save us!'

Sandy grinned. This was Gloria's game. She was a second-generation Londoner and secretary to the local race relations committee. There was a squeal, a puppy flew out into the garden, and Gloria swatted a passing infant. She was talking about Derek-Mohammed's temporary job in the supermarket. Sandy basked. He should ring his mother on the island. Idly he twined his fingers with Dora's. The kitchen was warm and Gloria's voice ripe and kind. Sandy was seized by an illumination that struck him as absurdly startling: that of the simplicity of happiness.

'Who was that? I heard the telephone. Pull the curtains. The light's too bright. Who was that telephoning?' Oliver turned his face away from the window and covered his eyes with his hand, spying through his fingers at Virginia.

'It's a sunny day. It'll do you good. Father, did you write to Sandy? How did you know his address?'

'Sent it care of your mother.'

'Well, he's coming.'

'So I should think. Where's my breakfast?'

'He's come all the way from Rome.'

Oliver sniffed. That damn sun made him sneeze.

Sandy was rolling his sleeping-bag.

'I don't want to go.'

'Your mother said there was no need.'

'I have to. You don't.'

Dora's packing was as minimal as his.

'I do. I want to see your island. What *is* it like?'

'Granny told you.'

'Not much.'

Sandy frowned. 'Someone once said it was anything you imagined it to be. So you tell me.'

'Ah, well.' Dora flopped back on the bed, resting her head on her hands. She was at her prettiest like this—happily pensive. In fact, she was altogether a more cheerful girl than people gave her credit for. 'Rivers of honey? Silver trees? No? Well, it must be something extraordinary, the way you all go on about it. Or in your case, don't.'

'It's just a place. Holiday camps. Too many trippers in summer. Yacht clubs, two lifeboats. When they were short of maps of Singapore in the war they used the island—it's the same shape.'

Dora shrugged. She was not too concerned about tomorrow: a quality Sandy envied. Sometimes, indeed, he wondered if that was why he was drawn to her, hoping that he might swim in her carefree wake from one day to the next. He himself gave the same impression, he knew, but it was spurious. Appearing to move lightly through life, Sandy stepped into the gutter to skirt a ladder, counted magpies, threw salt over his shoulder and wondered anxiously what would become of him. His parents felt the same, of course, and he wished sometimes that they would behave with less bemused tolerance on Sam's part and suppressed irritation on Virginia's. He wished someone would tell him what to do.

He should have rung his father while he was in London, he knew. But he could not imagine what they would have to say to each other. When Sandy was a child, they had a language, father and son. Now, on the rare occasions they met, they groped for a common speech.

'Sorry, what did you say?'

Dora repeated her question. 'Why did your grandparents split up?'

'I don't know. I'm not sure anyone remembers.'

Downstairs Gloria was yelling at Derek-Mohammed, who rocked on his heels, grinning. Sandy and Dora slipped past in the narrow passage.

They hitched to the coast. At the last moment, on the ferry, the mist came down, so Dora stepped ashore not knowing at all what she might find.

5

*H*umble thought, I blame her myself. That is, I think
Mrs Kitty was a selfish woman. She led him a dance,
first on the island then gadding around Abroad. He
never should have married an overer—they don't settle.

Not that they didn't make a handsome pair, I'll give
you that. She was very small, you know, and pretty
enough even with her black hair cut very short. They
called it cropped. My mam said you couldn't tell the lads
from the lasses.

I don't know that much about that part Abroad,
except it went on a long time. When the old reverend
threw away their postcards I used to pinch them from
the dustbin and hide them from my mam to look at
when I wanted. Later I stuck them in the album with
my name on the front: Susan Humble. There are other
private things in it, too. A pressed daisy a travelling
man once gave me, a school report for being tidy and
clean, a programme from when I went with my mam
to the Pier Follies, some recipes for being cured by
herbs—horehound for a cough, agrimony, colt's-foot

and hyssop. They're on the telly now but I don't believe they ought. My mam said always, too strong and you'll kill, not cure. I know them but I don't bother with them much.

There's a photo too, with the postcards. The two of them with that friend of his from the university, Mr Stephens. They're in some square in Venice and there's a blur in the air of birds' wings—pigeons, I'd say.

That's one place I'll go, if there's a package.

'Trevelyan! Can't beat him.'

'He was wrong about Piltdown man.'

'Along with the rest of the world.' Oliver blew his nose, thrashed among his papers and thrust a book at Virginia, with the page marked. 'Read that. Aloud. Read to me. Eyes tired.' He closed his eyes and composed himself as a child might, waiting for a story.

' "For many centuries after Britain became an island the untamed forest was king. Its moist and mossy floor was hidden from heaven's eye by a close-drawn curtain woven of innumerable tree-tops, which shivered in the breezes of summer dawn and broke into wild music of millions upon millions of wakening birds; the concert was prolonged from bough to bough with scarcely a break for hundreds of miles over hill and plain and mountain . . ." ' Virginia paused but he had not fallen asleep; his beckoning forefinger signalled impatiently: go on, go on. ' ". . . unheard by man save where, at rarest intervals, a troop of skin-clad hunters, stone-axe in hand, moved furtively over the ground beneath, ignorant that they lived upon an island, not dreaming that there could be other parts of the world besides this damp green woodland with its meres and marshes, wherein they hunted, a terror to its four-footed inhabitants and themselves afraid."'

Virginia nodded. It was beautiful, but she was wondering about Sandy. After the telephone call she had heard no more. Now he was coming she must stay, she told herself, and said the same to Sam.

'It's a year since we've seen him.'

'He knows where we live.'

Virginia bit her lip. 'Why don't you and Lucy come over for the weekend? It's lovely. Summer's still here.'

'I've a client on Saturday, site meeting. Come home when you're ready.'

He rang off. Virginia had not even spoken to Lucy.

Oliver was asleep.

Oliver was a hunter in the rectory rhododendrons. The figures of his mother and his nurse calling on the lawn were reduced to agitated dolls, the outside cat (strictly a mouser) promoted to a sabre-toothed tiger. Which, in dream, it truly was, and, as the leaves shuffled, the green-gold coins of light snapped into fearful eyes, the boy choked at the meaty, feral breath and called but was not answered and was not answered, for nightmare blocked his throat.

'Mama!'

Virginia paused, her hand on the door-knob.

'Did you say something?'

Oliver's eyes were blank.

'Eh?' He wore the stunned-owl expression with which he often wakened nowadays. He fumbled for his handkerchief and wiped his eyes—not from tears but rheum. Though something had shaken him. For a moment he seemed not to recognise his daughter.

'You must have been dreaming.'

'Ah. Been thinking a lot, lying here.'

'You shouldn't brood.'

'Never mind that.' He changed subject with the abruptness that characterised his conversation nowadays. 'Remember Ralph Stephens? Mag's godfather, pretty wife Angela?'

'Oh yes—he had a house for the summers at the Bar, didn't he? That's all I remember. And very small feet! Can't think how I know that—perhaps I saw him dancing. Why? Have you heard from him? Oh Lord! You've sent him a telegram too, haven't you?'

Almost primly, for him, Oliver answered. 'I may ask my own friend to my own house, I assume? I daresay I shan't be troubling any of you much longer. Now where's that woman?'

'Humble? She may have gone home but I might catch her. If she's there I'll send her up with your tea.'

Virginia watched Humble climb the stairs carrying the tray; laced black shoes and opaque support stockings. She heard a knock, her father's voice, and the sound of the bedroom door shutting.

56

'Lock the door.'

'Oh, Sir Oliver, I'm not so sure . . .'

'Pass the Milpar, Humble, and lock the door.'

'Damn.' A bramble caught Dora's cardigan. 'Are you sure you know the way?'

'Just hold on to me.' Sandy walked with one hand for Dora, the other groping ahead, as a blind man might test the path with his stick.

'How will that help if you don't know where you're going? I thought England didn't have fog any more.'

'It's not fog, it's sea mist. Can't you hear the light-house foghorn?'

'Sounds like the death-pangs of a dinosaur. Something in terrible pain.' Dora tripped and gasped. 'Let's sit down for a minute.'

Her nose was red, her knee-length cardigan sodden with the damp air, her hair hung like seaweed from under the rain-hat. Sandy was perplexed. Against his better judgment, he had brought her to the island and now he had lost them both. We are lost, he thought, the words dull and desolate in his head—for a moment he quite relished the weather's doomful echo in his mind. Then came the grind of a car and as they pressed themselves into the hedgerow, fog-lamps ripped a brief hole in the mist.

'I think if we cut through that field.' In the wake of the car they were blinder than before. Sandy sounded more resolute than he felt. 'Yes, I'm sure that's it. We used to pick mushrooms here. There'll be masses now, I expect.'

'Wouldn't it be better to stick to the road?'

'That goes miles round by the abbey.'

'Oh look! I've found a mushroom! Ouch, there are thistles too.' Dora sucked her finger. She crouched on her haunches reaching all round her. 'They're every-where, masses of them. I can feel them. It's extraordinary, like being blind. Shall we pick some?'

'Not just now. They might be toadstools anyway.'

'You said they were mushrooms.'

'That was years ago.'

They stumbled on in silence and darkness. Are we having a row? Sandy wondered. With Dora one could never be sure. She expressed anger in silence, yet, equally, silence could mean preoccupation with some-thing or, just as often, with nothing at all. In a fashion Sandy admired, Dora could actually empty her mind. He even imagined it empty, as an untinted bone china bowl—if you held it up, the light would shine through.

'What's that?'

'What?'

'That wet pulling noise.'

'Cows eating grass. Have you never been to the country?'

'Not really. Not for longer than an afternoon. I think I've just walked through a cow turd.'

'Pat.'

'What?'

'Never mind.' Sandy began to find it amazingly

tiring—searching out a path and at the same time talking. 'Wait a minute.' He stood still and sniffed the air. He could hear cows breathing around them and one coughed. The herd seemed to be moving with them. 'I can smell the sea but it's not where it should be. Hold on, I'll light a match. Wish we had a torch.' Sandy was suddenly alarmed. 'Dora? Where are you? Stop fooling around.' The match went out, but not before he had glimpsed Dora disappearing over the edge of the cliff. There was a scraping, rattling sound and the cows edged back a little, dribbling and chewing. Dora was clinging grimly to a bush that turned out on inspection to be gorse.

'Oh, my poor love!'

'It's only my hands really. The prickles from that bush.'

'The cliffs are frightfully dangerous—the whole island's sliding into the sea. And it's all my fault, that you fell over I mean.'

They were sitting a few yards back from the edge in a necessarily awkward embrace—Dora's palms could not be touched, spiked as they were with needles of gorse. A puff of breeze from the south-west cleared the mist, revealing a thin, lazy moon on her back, a flat silver sea and Dora: with her hair even wilder, her face scratched and bleeding, a striking figure. But for the elastic that had slipped from her chin to her neck, she would have lost her rain-hat.

In that moment of illumination Sandy—who had never quite known what love was though he knew it to be infinitely desired—wondered if he might be in love with Dora. If it were love to want to take the pain of another upon yourself, then he certainly was—he would gladly have endured the agony of her thorns in his skin, to relieve her. He took a deep breath to speak, but before he could declare himself the moon went in again and the time was gone.

Half an hour later, they sat in the rectory kitchen. While Virginia made them sandwiches and coffee Sandy used tweezers to draw the gorse needles from Dora's palms.

'There. Shall I get some Dettol?'

'I'll just wash them.'

'Are you sure?' Her hands were badly cut, too, and Sandy had picked out grit as well as thorns. Thinking of tetanus, he was alarmed, seized by visions of Dora with lock-jaw, carried off, Dora dying, a world without Dora. Since, as a child, he had imagined his parents dead, himself a grieving orphan, Sandy had never felt such irrational terror for anyone (proof of passion, surely?); and the orphan thing had been an infantile, hysterical fantasy—one of several ploys to induce the divine and secret luxury of tears. He subdued his panic for Dora, not at all sure how she would take it. 'There's a proper sink down the passage. And a loo.'

Virginia put down the plate of sandwiches.

'Well, I'll go back to bed.'

'Yes. Sorry we got you up.' Sandy felt awkward. He took the chance while Dora was out of the room: 'I hope it's all right, Ma—about Dora, I mean.'

'Of course.'

'She wanted to come. To see the island.'

'You must show it to her then.'

Sandy nodded, then remembered. 'How is Grand-father?'

Virginia reflected. 'I honestly don't know. He won't have the doctor and I can't tell. There's nothing speci-fic—except age, I suppose.'

She stood, arms wrapped around her, in her smart, severe dressing-gown that seemed out of place here, in this house, this kitchen that was the warm heart of the house. Watching Sandy eat, she thought: this is my son I have not seen for a year, this young adult is flesh of my flesh, familiar and yet alien with his thin wiry wrists, that scar I have not noticed before—a little crescent of white skin near the eye.

When he arrived they had brushed cheeks in the hall. Now, standing behind him, Virginia reached with her hand to touch his shoulder and, at the last moment, hearing steps in the passage, withdrew it. She stood aside for Dora to come in. 'Good night then.'

'Night, Ma.'

The weird girl smiled. Virginia went slowly upstairs, abstracted, hand trailing the banister rail. Flora was it? Or Dora? Floradora? She smiled, began to hum to herself: Floradora, how I adora.

'My things were all wet so I put this on. I hope that's all right. It was hanging in the loo.'

Dora was wearing a cast-off dressing-gown of Oliver's, Jaeger vintage 1935, dog-brown and dried-blood check, with mud-coloured revers and tasselled cord. She dragged a good yard of train behind her and when she dropped her hands her arms disappeared.

Sandy grinned. 'It was my grandfather's. It looks fantastic. So do you. All pink.'

'There was a nailbrush. I scrubbed my face.'

She ignored the place at the table and sank into a rocking-chair by the stove—the seat in which Humble usually chose to drink her tea.

'How are your hands?' She turned them palms upwards and Sandy took them in his. 'Do they hurt?'

'A bit. But that bush probably saved my life.'

'I suppose it did.'

He brought the sandwiches and sat at her feet. It seemed extraordinary to have Dora here, in the house, on the island—as though someone had drawn a perfect circle around his circumstances and said: there, just for this moment, you have all you desire, the person and the place. Immediately he was afraid. What a risk to acknowledge bliss! Might as well ask to have it snatched away.

In spite of her painful hands, Dora had made her way effectively through the food and now sank back.

'What's he like?'

'Who?'

'Your grandfather, of course.' She pulled the dressing-gown more tightly around her.

'Oh, I don't know. You'll see him if you want to but you probably won't. Apparently he doesn't get up any more. A bit of a pest. A bit of an eccentric.' Sandy considered. 'When I was small, I thought he was a magician. Did good tricks.' He rested his head on Dora's lap. 'Grannie once described him as "a man of infirm purpose"—I remember now. They had all these cats and when they split up there was a fuss about who was to keep them—have custody. Grannie was going abroad, so she lost.'

Dora yawned. 'Are we going to be in the same room?'

This question had not occurred to Sandy. They had shared a bed—or a mattress or a floor—for so long he could not imagine sleeping without Dora. Literally sleeping, for that matter: a pleasure that had surprised Sandy the first time it happened.

'Yes,' he said firmly, 'in my room.'

'Good.'

In the corridor she whispered: 'Where's your grandfather?'

'Up there. In the tower.'

'A real tower?' He nodded. 'Heaven!' Dora smiled the wide smile she reserved for delight at the appropriateness of things.

One pilchard, a chocolate cup-cake, a barley-sugar, two ounces of Danish blue, mostly rind, and a nip of Sanatogen tonic wine. Oliver pulled a face: not the best of dormitory feasts, but pickings were trickier to hoard with Ginny around. He pushed the biscuit-tin back under the bed and teased Alcestis with the pilchard before biting it in half; she didn't care for the tomato sauce and shook her whiskers. She was right, Oliver thought—or perhaps it didn't go with the cup-cake? He swallowed a tooth-mug full of tonic wine to take away the taste. Disgusting stuff. Get Humble to top up the Milpar bottle with whisky tomorrow—stores in a bad way all round.

Two a.m. Strategy against constipation and bedsores: out of bed and twelve times round the deck; bend, stretch, bend, stretch. Surgical spirit for the buttocks, cream for piles and sit out for a while by the gas fire. Cold at night now—autumn of course, the cats told him that, complaining to stay in. His bones too; the young knew nothing of it, how the nerves turned traitor, sending messages of pain from limb to limb. Lie down and the heart crashed out its own wilful beat, while within, the spirit fretted—still young, still waiting to begin.

The voyages with Humble are a relief.

And any mischief I can make.

He dozed. He dreamed. As Kitty did on a warmer shore. She murmured and tossed on the seas of nightmare; the island shifting, changing shape, Protean—now Leviathan rising, now rock upon which she might break, be wrecked. She half-woke, sank back, and then suddenly it was the loveliest dream of small craft on calm water in a soft breeze, with spinnakers the colours of butterfly wings, each dipping then filling her single wing as she ran before the scented wind.

'How pretty. Olly, look!' Kitty spoke aloud, startling her cat.

Sandy smiled in his sleep at the pretty colours.

Virginia was the island, or the island had possessed her: it was the shape of a woman kneeling in the water, face touching the sea, hair spread by the tide, the woman helpless, in danger of drowning. She woke gasping. The rain had stopped.

In Sussex, Oliver's friend, Ralph Stephens, owner of a Jack Russell, widower, a neat man with small feet good for dancing, pink complexion and disciplined moustache, slept less well than usual. There was music in his head, a wild tune his feet could not follow, but he danced and danced all night.

Dora did not dream at all.

It was Ralph who had found Oliver and Kitty the house at St Marie-la-Douce, that year of their travels after Margaret's birth. Oliver's friend at Oxford and later in the Foreign Office, he had come often to the island and after the war bought a house at the Bar. At the time of the Hartleys' journeyings he was doing well. After several postings he was a second secretary in Rome with an eye on the Paris plum—Hitler permitting, for this was 1938. Angela would have liked Paris. A languid, elegant girl, tall, with a sharp, witty nose, she made an unlikely mate for dapper little good-hearted Ralph, who gave the appearance not so much of a diplomat, as of a soldier in mufti.

So Oliver and Kitty rested and walked for a while in the French countryside and by the time they reached Venice, to meet Ralph, Kitty had very nearly recovered her strength and spirits. Cities still tired her though, and something about the searching, wavering water-light of Venice alarmed her. While Oliver stalked in long, stiff strides from church to church to palace to island, in company with a battered Ruskin, Kitty confessed to Ralph as the bells boiled in her head and pigeons rose in gusts around the belfries—heraldic birds against a hard sky—'I think I must leave.'

Ralph touched his moustache, laid a hand briefly on Kitty's, and carried the Hartleys off to the hill village in the rocks above Menton. In those days there was no craft shop or expatriate community, no boutique, no vegetarian restaurant, only one minimal food shop. While not actually hostile, the natives regarded the newcomers warily, would fall silent as they passed and gossip furiously in their wake. The road up in Ralph's small open Ford was tortuous and exhausting. The first morning they woke to fog and flies. Kitty adored it. Oliver went off to survey the relic of a Saracen fort and pronounced it inferior. For love of Kitty he bought the house, so he said. He never came there again, except in dream or in his journeys *ex corpore*. Then, he would swoop on a northerly gale across the Channel, through thunder-storms in northern France, coast on the thermals as the sky cleared and hover on a warm-milk morning above St Marie-la-Douce to catch, if he were lucky, a glimpse of Kitty at breakfast on her terrace. He could never alight, but once dived low and close enough for his breath to mist an apricot on a creamy white dish.

But not tonight, when dreams were spiked and horned, then frightful as the great sea-worms of story that rose, waving their lichened heads, had him in their coils to tug and draw below, beneath the sea, down, to drown.

Then a violent surfacing to shocking light.

Virginia rattled back the curtains.

'Lovely day. It's the weekend. Sandy's here. Whatever's that smell? Fish? Have the cats brought something in?'

Oliver groaned. He did look rather awful: a bad colour, his eyes were gummy and the sheets twisted as though he had been tossing in his sleep. Today she had been determined to get him up but now she was not so sure.

'Are you all right, Father?'

His hand fluttered feebly.

'Stomach. Bad night.'

Virginia put down the tea-cup, surveyed him doubtfully and reached to straighten the sheet. Abruptly angry and at once ashamed, she thought: Pippa's good at this sort of thing—why can't she do it? Then her hand brushed his and there was some small memory of the flesh to pierce her—one of his casual kindnesses, a hand to steady her when she fell? Something from childhood. But then another thought, uncalled-for: he crippled me.

67

Maybe I've crippled Sandy. Perhaps that's how it is, what we always do? Sam and I, all those years congratulating ourselves that Sandy had somehow miraculously vaulted the horrors of adolescence! He never even had acne—just a few spots on his back, but seemed blessedly destined to slip from sweet-natured child to adult. You couldn't say he actually rebelled. He simply walked away from us, from college, closing the door behind him with a firm courtesy worse and more final than anger.

'Is there anything you want? I do think the doctor—'

'Just send Humble up when she comes.'

'She's not here. It's a Saturday. I told her not to come.'

Outrage. Drooping lip. She could have sworn he was going to burst into tears of petulance.

'Sandy's brought a girl. They got here late last night or he'd have come in to see you.'

'Girl? What sort of girl?'

'Dora. A bit odd but could be worse.' Virginia twitched the curtain. 'Oh, there she is in the garden—wearing your old dressing-gown. The Jaeger one. She's standing on the lawn. She's bending down. Alcestis seems to have taken to her—how extraordinary, she never likes strangers. I'll get you some Bisodol.'

Oliver had brightened.

'I daresay I could manage a bit of bacon.'

'Are you sure that's a good idea?'

'Got to keep going. A bit of bacon then I might have a shave.'

But when the bacon came, Oliver could not face it after all. Perhaps he had kept that pilchard too long? Or it might have been the Danish blue. He offered it to the gang but, as usual, it was his Alcestis of the swift paw who won. She retreated with her booty to the top of the wardrobe, opening her mouth in silent hiss as a warning to challengers; knowing herself unchallenged for she alone could make the leap from chest to wardrobe top. Oliver had observed before that in cats mental and physical agility frequently came together. A pity the same could not be said of people.

His bowels warned, and now with unfeigned stiffness he left his bed, made his way precariously along the passage and even more painfully up the short winding flight of stairs to his turret-top lavatory. Mahogany seat, box base and lid; a dressing-gown cord to replace the old chain; heap of dusty books—some rubbish Oliver had bought on railway journeys and had been known to use as lavatory paper, also Jack London, Conrad, Kipling, Augustine, old friends and foes.

Oliver sat on, book in hand, the lid down, recovering himself, surveying from his throne the three little pictures—like a triptych—yielded by the narrow Gothic windows that made up one jutting half of the tower. A shining sea, the waves curling just enough to break, Saturday dinghy race round Deadhorse buoy and a great three-master on a beam reach: a well-found ship for a true voyage. *O Lord God, grant us peace, for all that we have is your gift. Grant us the peace of repose, the peace of the Sabbath, the peace which has no evening. For this worldly order in all its beauty will pass away. All these things that are very good will come to an end when the limit of their existence is reached.*

Old sourpuss saint! Sainted lecher who wrote like God if the Lord could write. If the Lord. You think I haven't listened for the voice of the child in the nearby house? Oliver flung down the book, startled by grief so that he brought his hands to his face and the tears ran through his fingers. St Augustine lay on the floor, his spine broken, while Oliver gasped, mopped his eyes with his dressing-gown sleeve and, reaching in his pocket for a Woodbine, pondered his outburst. The only sin— he had said once, strolling with Ralph in the embassy garden in Damascus (was it? or Rome?)—the only sin to oneself is regret. Shun it and thou shalt be free from guilt. From sorrow, too, for that which is lost or will soon be taken, he would now have added: for the scene before him, for a summer afternoon in a boat with Kitty, much history he had read and a little he had written, some women he had loved (in particular a chancellery typist in wartime Cairo who walked most delicately on his back—remedially and erotically—while playing a flute); the certainty of a merciful God mislaid at the age of five, the scent of the island from seaward five miles off, his first cat that had died. Still, from time to time, the present—when there was the feel of a new book, unread, a good bowel movement, some mischief to be done.

Well, there may still be something before we go forth. A bright day.

When, at last, Oliver returned to his room there was a young female sitting in the high-backed fireside chair, with Alcestis in her lap.

Affronted, Oliver blew his nose.

'Hello,' she said. 'I'm Dora Phenicule. I came with Sandy. Are you going to get up?'

6

Kitty looked through her wardrobe: nothing at all to travel in. Should she take that for an omen? Besides, what did one wear nowadays for a journey, she wondered aloud in the boutique where all the clothes seemed to her quite extraordinary. Designed for gypsies perhaps—all these shawls and sequins and bangles and fringes; tiny bracelets that appeared large enough for a baby's wrist; baggy trousers drawn in with elastic somewhere below the knee. In summer the place was packed with a Babel of trippers up from the coast but today, towards the end of the season, the Swedish girl who owned both the craft shop and boutique had banished her assistants for the winter and—wearing shorts and a smock, with her hair plaited in a pigtail—was up a ladder painting the wall. Her baby lay naked on the floor, waving his legs.

'Oh, I am sorry, we are almost closing.'

Kitty considered backing out, but then she thought of the frightfulness of the journey down the hill to shop, even if she could get a lift. And then Menton! It used to be such fun but now they had built those flats on the front it seemed to Kitty a terrible place.

'Something,' she said, 'for a journey. Unless you are closed?'

She thought: I am behaving distractedly, as though I had already set out, anticipating the shock of turning the key in the lock and leaving my house. How can I ever do it?

When she cared to use it, the girl had the most beautiful smile. She had only a slight accent—American, not Swedish, though the inflections were Scandinavian.

'No, I mean I am sorry about the mess. You are going far?'

'England.'

The girl considered her gravely, with the air of a doctor. Kitty felt she had made a mistake. Suddenly short of breath, she wondered whatever she was doing here when she could have been lying in the shady corner of her terrace. She was not used to shopping for anything larger than a daily salad, bread, small household needs—life's teaspoons and egg-cups. She made to turn away from the girl's scrutiny, seeing herself a clumsy old woman; besides, even if she were to go, what about puss? How could she trust Minette to anyone?

'I think perhaps another time—'

'Oh, we are not busy; this is the best time.'

'But the clothes. They are very pretty. I don't feel I could wear them.' It seemed at that moment an impossible journey. Kitty had travelled so much in her life and yet this one small trip threatened, as though the structure of her existence here in this safe place were so fragile it might not survive her departure.

'But yes, look! This one is very simple and you are so slim. Jersey, you see, with a little synthetic. It will not crease. Not too hot in winter here and in England now, just right.'

Behind the screen—there was no changing room— Kitty surveyed herself, smoothed her hair, turned round to look at the hem. Perhaps? At least this one wasn't fancy dress. Very simple, certainly smarter than anything she had in her wardrobe. The colour—not one she would ever have chosen nowadays—was a clear, bold blue.

'Come to the door. There is a mirror. You can see it in the light.'

But if she did not go, whenever would she wear it?

'You are so lucky to go to England.'

Kitty had almost forgotten the girl was there.

'You like England?'

'Oh, yes! It is so soft. The country is like a dream.'

Yes, Kitty thought, from exile that is how it seems: the nuisances, the drabness, the wearying self-evisceration fade, and in their place this vision, a dream of England as kind and beautiful as earth seen from space.

'I'm afraid I am going on family matters. It may not be possible though —it might be for some time and I don't like to leave my cat.'

'But I will have her! Or I will come to your house and feed her. My little boy and I have often seen her. That would be nothing. In the winter I have not enough to do.'

And so, apparently, it was settled. Somehow, in the short time it had taken to buy a dress, the Swedish girl had made Kitty tremulously brave to go. Walking away with her parcel, she looked back and saw mother and son in the doorway. The child was hoisted to shoulder level to wave to the old English lady.

Virginia had put on the steak and kidney to simmer while she made the pastry. She felt awkward using someone else's kitchen, inept with the wooden rolling-pin she remembered from childhood. For that matter whose kitchen was it? Certainly not hers or her mother's. Humble's, she supposed. She paused, her back aching, and looked out at the shining day: the shawl of silver webs slung between the yew and the quince. At home, in London, on a morning like this, they would sleep late, shop quickly, eat at a McDonald's—Lucy's heaven—and spend a long afternoon on the heath. In summer sometimes they swam in the ponds: so cold, so green, so dark, so deep, that Virginia found them faintly alarming—one of a wilder Nature's orifices in the midst of the polite urban park. (Not that anyone in their right minds walked alone in the less frequented stretches of the heath nowadays, but that was man's indecency to man.)

So that was Virginia's idea of their Saturdays: a picture, as simple as a child's drawing, of Sam and herself swinging across the grass, hand in hand, while Lucy ran ahead calling a friend, a dog. From a distance her life seemed as wonderfully uncomplicated and achievable as had Sam's vision of a new world twenty years ago when all was to be redrawn on the back of envelopes according to the gospel of St Corbusier. And modular men of the new city were to dwell in tower blocks and *Terrassenhäuser*, while Sam, along with most of their architect friends, ended up in a comfortable converted Victorian villa within reach of a park.

Perhaps, Virginia pondered as she dusted the pin with flour to roll the pastry again, it was absence that ironed out the wrinkles in life; look closer and a cold wind drives the family from the heath.

Now, for a year, Sandy had been missing from the picture, faded out as by a cinematic trick; one moment rolling down the hill, yelling with joy, knees of his jeans green-stained, the next all legs and elbows, kicking a stone as he trailed behind them. Then she glanced over her shoulder and abruptly he was gone. She had yet to recognise the stranger upstairs.

The pastry was too thick but it would have to do: if she rolled it thinner it would fall apart. Putting it in the oven, she made up her mind, rinsed her hands quickly under the tap and went to the study, shutting the door behind her. She drummed her finger-tips on the desk, willing them to answer.

'Lucy? Hello, darling.'

Lucy must have run to the telephone—she was breathless.

'I'm going to get a puppy.'

'Well, yes, we can talk about that. Daddy and I will talk about it. Is he there? Lucy?'

'We're going now. Sarah's mother's going to give us one. I can choose. When are you coming back, Mum?'

'Lucy, I said before, I don't really think a puppy— will you get Daddy?'

'Are you coming today?'

'No, sweetie. I can't. Grandpa isn't very well. Now please call Daddy.'

'Ginny?'

'Sam. It's such a lovely weekend, I thought you might. Oh, I'd forgotten. The site meeting.'

'When are you coming home, Ginny?'

'Soon. Not sure.'

'Whyever can't Pippa cope?'

'Sam, what's all this about a puppy?'

'They take advantage of you.'

'I've been through this with Lucy—we cannot keep a puppy in London.'

'He's a hypochondriac, you know that.'

'In any case, she's not old enough to be responsible for a dog. Who's going to walk it every day?'

'Mrs Humble's perfectly competent to look after Oliver. I miss you, Ginny.'

'You can never leave a dog. We've got to talk about this properly.'

'Come home, Virginia.'

Sam cut her off. Still holding the receiver, Virginia realised she had not told him that Sandy was here.

Opening the study door, she was startled by a figure in the dim hall.

'Mrs Humble! I hadn't expected you. It's Saturday.'

'I thought as you had people.'

'Well, bless you, yes. But honestly we're under control.'

The woman seemed disinclined to leave. She stood there, her feet in the black laced shoes adamant not to budge, her gaze behind the circular spectacles tipped towards the stairs in the attitude of an attentive seagull.

Virginia said more firmly, 'Truly, Mrs Humble. It's only Sandy and a friend.'

Doubtfully, Humble turned at last. 'Well then, if you really think.'

'I'm sure. Off you go. Thank you.' To reinforce her point, Virginia opened the front door and watched Humble down the path and out of sight. Only when she had closed the door did it occur to her: how did Humble know that anyone had come?

The island was melting gold, fluid; gold fruit hung from the trees, the stubble was fired by the light and so was Dora's hair as she sat at Oliver's window. He thought she looked like someone and, startled, said so.

'Modigliani's mistress? The last one?' Dora said.

'Eh? Who? Not that I know of. A girl once, some-where.' He was exhausted. And now this female barging into his room calling up someone lost. They were like ghosts, these revenants—and most troubling were the women: the loved, the rejected, the half-remembered, the turn of a girl's shoulder, the slope of a woman's hip. This mist of wraiths from other lives teased him, as a soft breath on his cheek, laughter from another room. Tears too! Oh, what man would come into this world again to the keening of women, that lake of salt! A Dead Sea.

When he could still get about Oliver would follow a woman in a city street for a glimpse of a cheek, only to meet a gaze faintly remembered, in a stranger's face.

And so astonishing it was that he—old Cronus regarding Dora's crossed ankles with appreciation—should still cling so to each incarnation, gasping to the end for love like a new-born infant for milk.

'Who d'you say? This painter's woman?'

'Jeanne Hébuterne. When he died she threw herself from the window at dawn. Don't you think that was remarkable? It was the fifth floor.' As Dora talked, Alcestis (standoffish normally with strangers) was indulging in unusual intimacies: she lay coiled and draped on Dora's neck and shoulder like one of the tippets women used to affect. Her fur almost exactly matched Dora's hair.

'The fifth floor, eh?'

Dora nodded.

'And why did she do that?'

'Because he asked her to follow him. She was his favourite model. He wanted her with him in Paradise.'

Oliver grunted, but something disturbed him, like a draught from a door left open. Back in bed, he closed his

79

eyes. When he opened them again the intrusive child was still there—not so easily banished.

'Why don't you get up?'

'Because I choose not to. This is my death-bed.'

Dora surveyed him not unkindly but with apparent dispassion. 'Are you frightened? Would you like me to sit with you?' Oliver sighed, although he was not altogether displeased. 'As you wish. If you could manage to be quiet.'

'Oh, I don't usually talk very much.'

Dora sat on in the window-seat, content enough, the warm cushion of Alcestis on her lap. After half an hour Sandy put his head round the door. She tipped the cat gently to the ground and left the room.

Oliver slept on. He dreamed of diving upwards out of a window into golden air, with an angel at his heels.

Taking off at Nice was terrifying. Kitty was convinced the aircraft would fall into the sea. She shut her eyes, but then was confronted by the re-run scene of parting from Minette, her precious Persian bundle, who had known perfectly well that she was to be abandoned and refused consolation. Then the helter-skelter drive down the mountain in the hire car wondering if Britt would remember about liver and fish or just serve up those awful tins Kitty felt sure were horse.

Silly old woman, Kitty told herself and, now they had levelled off and her stomach returned to its moorings, opened her eyes and surveyed the sea below. For a moment, looking out, she could have sworn she saw Olly, looking in. That was, of course, absurd—whatever would he be doing at twenty thousand feet? Kitty shook her head, unlatched her seat belt, let out a breath, slipped off her shoes (only the smallest heel and no laces), and dug in her straw bag for Barbara Pym and *Paris Match*. She was beginning to enjoy herself.

Virginia laughed. The pie had gone down well, she had left Oliver with Sandy and the girl for the afternoon, and now this evening's whisky was going down even better. Two before, one with, and now a topper for the washing-up (not her a bit really, but lately, since she came to the island, she had a feeling of a self that appeared and disappeared like the Cheshire Cat).

Flora-Dora, drying, repeated, 'OBE.'

'You mean my father's got a medal?' Sandy's paramour did appear marginally less weird through a seventy-per-cent-proof haze.

'No. It's called out-of-body experience. We were talking about it this afternoon.'

'My God! Here, come on. Tell me.' Virginia left the dishes and steered Dora to join Sandy by the fire and the whisky bottle. She filled her glass up to the top.

Virginia took the rocking-chair, Dora the high-backed carver. The cardigan and rain-hat had been exchanged for evening rig: high boots, and two bedspreads—one, precariously shackled with nappy-pins, serving as a skirt, the other, with a hole cut for the head, as a vaguely

Russian blouse. Her hair was more or less up in a conical chignon anchored in place by what appeared to be scrubbed, crossed bones.

'Go on.'

'Well, it's quite simple really. A lot of people have it. The soul leaves the body and roams at will. You can go anywhere you like but you tend to go upwards. I mean indoors you'd be somewhere on the ceiling; that's something to do with psycho-chemicals, the soul being lighter than air. Rather like NDE.'

The girl might have been explaining a train timetable.

'NDE?'

'Near-death-experience. I can't vouch for that, of course, as I've never been near death. Sir Oliver was very interesting on that.'

Worser and worser, thought Virginia.

'Whatever do you mean? Is he really dying?' She found it hard to believe she was having this conversation.

'Oh, I don't think so. But he's had so many reincarnations he can remember.'

Sandy spoke for the first time. 'I'll go and chop some wood.'

'Ah.' Virginia took another gulp. She found herself holding onto the arms of the chair, in fear of levitation. 'But you can vouch for the other thing—OBE?'

'Oh yes.' Dora smiled her rare and beautiful smile—all the more to be prized that it was discriminatingly bestowed. 'I took off once from the Battersea Heliport. It was beautiful—like flying without the fuss. There was a storm over the Mediterranean so I turned east. I'd never realised Japan was so small.' She spoke patiently, as though explaining to a child; or rather, to a marginally retarded adult, for a child would have understood. 'It's like a dream, but you know it's real and you can direct it. One of the best things is no jet lag—you leave your body behind, you see.'

'I suppose.'

'I think people have always been able to do it, they have just forgotten how. There's a legend in China of a tribal chieftain's wife, Chang E, who flew to the moon four thousand years ago. They said she had stolen an elixir, but I think it was OBE. She lived there with a woodcutter and a rabbit.'

'A rabbit?'

Dora smiled and nodded. Out of a Tesco plastic bag, she took a piece of dun-coloured knitting and wooden needles. Virginia watched her, hypnotised. Knit two, drop one, purl two, drop one.

'What are you making?'

'Nothing. I can't afford the wool. But I like knitting, you see.'

'Absolutely.'

'It's very kind of you to have me here. I love it. I could stay for ever.'

Virginia found she was nodding in time with the dropped stitches. Perhaps it was the heat from the fire, but she felt much drunker than she normally would on two large whiskies. It was an effort to keep her eyes open.

'Where do you live, Dora? I mean normally?'

'With Sandy.' Knit two.

'No, I mean before?'

'London. Anywhere. Italy. I was doing art history. It's what everyone does nowadays who isn't very clever.' Drop one.

'I'd have thought you were quite clever.'

Dora pondered this for a moment, with the stitch to be knitted precariously poised at the tip of the needle. She worked like a Frenchwoman with the needles lodged somewhere up in her armpits, and like a child—tongue sticking out, each stitch painfully achieved.

'Oh no. I have an intuitive imagination, that's all.' Drop two. The spell was broken.

'Is Dora by any chance taking a hallucinatory drug?' Virginia asked Sandy. He seemed shocked.

'She won't even touch aspirin. Why?'

'I just wondered.'

Oliver was frustrated. He had no inclination to get up, yet curiosity about the goings-on downstairs (and something, he felt sure, was going on—hadn't that been half the point in getting them here?) prompted him to send his spirit out from his body. The catch was, he could only travel upwards, and by the time he reached the banisters at the top of the stairs, the damn thing was on the ceiling. All he could hear was a murmur of voices when someone left a door open.

Something else was bothering him. Nothing in his enquiries into the paranormal had indicated that this was likely or even possible but once or twice lately he had had the embarrassing impression that he was manifesting himself. He had dropped in on that chess tournament and could have sworn the Russian defector fellow spotted him: it was from that point on that the player lost his grip. And what had made Priam, the old tabby with the chewed ear, hiss and run like Hell on the roof yesterday? And now, this morning, Kitty in the plane—for a second she had looked puzzled and slightly alarmed.

Oliver scratched his bottom. Well, it would be out soon enough, he supposed, since he had told Sandy's young woman. Why he had told her he could not have explained—except that she was, literally, a kindred spirit—but the confession had brought him an unexpected sense of relief. Queer-looking, but there was something about her.

Not good times, these, for travel, unless you had a taste for violence. He could have told them, of course, there was nothing new about that: as in dream, old horrors returned to him. His most terrible death, by rabies, in the France of the Hundred Years' War; and then, another time, when he was the rat himself who fed the flea and brought the Dance of Death to a third of Europe—a great time for flagellants and Jew-haters. Idiot man, mistaking disaster for punishment, lashing himself from one dark age to the next. Now he does see, but learns nothing, so perhaps it is true, Alcestis my

85

dear: this is the darkest of all. And the joke is, you see, that God, that old warmonger, is abroad again, like the flea. His name, at least. If You are there, You sod, why do You let them use Your name? If You are not, my apologies.

I could tell them who killed John Kennedy.

To rise in this cosmic chain of being, I have read that one must strive for a good death. I burned at Rheims for You in the full expectation of freedom, that my spirit would at last go to You or to merciful nothingness. Only to be chucked into life again with debts and a foul-tempered wife.

Alcestis, my love, we must buy you a flea collar.

Sandy found it difficult to quarrel in his narrow single bed—there was so much Dora in it.

'Well, I don't see the point in staying.' His feet were cold but to warm them on Dora's would be to give in.

'But we must stay! What about your grandfather? He sent for you.'

'And he's hardly spoken to me since we got here.' Sandy would not turn to her, but gazed sternly at the ceiling. He was unable to explain why he was sulking, since he did not know.

'I think he's very interesting.'

'Apparently.'

'And so are you.'

'Dora.' A barn owl in the abbey copse woke and blinked at the moon. 'Dora, don't do that. Stop it. I don't feel like it.' A shrew would die tonight. 'Oh, Dora! Yes! Christ! Dora!'

In the morning, on the ferry, Kitty looked again at the set of a man's shoulders. He was shortish but very straight-backed; small feet. Hair white now, of course. It couldn't be and then it almost certainly was.

'Kitty, my dear!'

'Ralph! I'd have known you anywhere.'

'And this is Jackie.'

Kitty looked round, then down. The dog for the man, without a doubt, it had the Jack Russell air of optimism and busyness. She hoped it wouldn't bark. Ralph had never been a cat man, she recalled: such a pity but then she could see, he wasn't the build or temperament. If he had been a dog, he would have barked—cheerfully. They both spoke at the same moment.

'You haven't changed.'

'Friends don't.' Kitty smiled and laid her hand on his wrist. Then she remembered. 'You haven't had a telegram, too? Oh dear.'

'To tell you the truth, I didn't know what to make of it. Bothered me a bit, so I thought I'd better come.'

Kitty nodded. 'We always did what Olly said, didn't we? Still, that's nice—we can arrive together. I was frightened of the journey, you know, but really I've rather enjoyed it.'

As they stood together at the forward end of the vessel (hardly bows, in this push-me-pull-you ferry),

Kitty glanced at Ralph's profile and thought, such a *good* man. Why is wickedness always so attractive?

The mist had cleared. It was calm. Flakes of sunlight on the water dazzled. The island had been pickled in amber.

Here they were. They had arrived.

7

'A place of worship of some kind. Or sacrifice.' Virginia, hands pushed deep in pockets and collar up, shouted into the wind. 'This was the last place in England to be converted to Christianity.'

Sandy knew, of course. She wished he wouldn't stand so close to the cliff edge. Dora, whom she was addressing, stalked around the massive weathered stone at the topmost point of Poet's Walk. Here the cliffs were at their highest and most precipitous, falling almost vertically to the rocks below where—twenty yards from the shore—two tides met and boiled in a race.

'It's got a lap,' said Dora, completing her tour of the stone, and sat in it, facing out to sea. The wind blew up the brim of her rain-hat and, but for the elastic, would have snatched it away.

'That's why it's called Cerdic's throne, but actually it's supposed to be pre-Saxon. No one knows much about it though everyone has their own idea. I can't believe it was for Druid sacrifice because there could never have been a sacred grove here—trees simply wouldn't survive.' Indeed, where they stood nothing grew but greyish salt-chewed grass and a couple of stunted gorse bushes. 'There are all kinds of stories about it, of course.'

'Magic.' Sandy startled them, they had forgotten him. He tossed something from his pocket into the foam below, where quarrelling currents created a whirlpool. Even from this height they could hear the moan and crack of the tide in an unseen cave, as though the sea had accepted his offering. This little ritual performed, he stepped back from the edge and squatted at Dora's feet. Automatically Virginia thought: he must be freezing without a coat.

Dora's eyes widened. 'What magic?'

Sandy shrugged. 'Ask Ma. She and Grandfather have been doing a history of the island for years.'

'You mean Grandfather has. I just look things up. Mostly, I can't find them. It seems to be a bit like those extraordinary stones in Cornwall—everyone has his theory, generally crackpot. There's a couple of references in the Anglo-Saxon Chronicle, and William of Malmesbury or one of his stooges. Something about a place of worship—*locus dei*—but that seems to have been a second thought. On the manuscript *dei* has been written over what looks like *magicus*.' She shivered. 'It's cold, let's start down. Isn't that Ralph Stephens? It must be—there's the dog.' Far below as a lark's plunge a figure was making its way across the softer, kinder fields.

'That's interesting,' said Dora. She hardly meant Ralph Stephens.

'Oh. Yes. Well, there are a few other references. Gildas says there was a shrine here but he's always unreliable. Over the centuries people have made it what they wanted—that's how it happens. Maybe because the island was overrun so often, it became known at one point as a site of last defence. It's higher than the Downs. Then when the Danes landed there was a story that a small number of natives held out here and, rather than give in, stepped off the cliffs. Then as their bodies were never found, it became popular legend that they didn't die but were mysteriously transported elsewhere.'

'UFOs,' Sandy said.

Virginia tied her headscarf more securely. As they stood, Dora's rain-hat was lifted by a gust (though thanks to the elastic, not lost) and her hair, crinkly as unravelled knitting wool, stood out all around her head.

'Anyhow, in the last war although the idea was clearly absurd, it was known as a place of safety. People came here in the raids. It's strange how folk-memory works. I was too young to remember but Humble told me.'

Dora lingered while Virginia and Sandy picked their way down. It was a relief to be out of the full force of the wind. Still—as Virginia thought to herself—there was something blessedly simplifying about real weather: intense heat, high wind, a thunder-storm. It dispelled the gnats of life, and although it could not vanquish the monsters, a great gale could hold them for a time at bay, being itself monstrous. In London, where one knew only that it was wet or dry, she missed this element. Not Sam, whose native heath was Hampstead; a city creature, his runs were narrow streets, his skyline roofs and chimney-pots and steeples and towers and domes.

'I like a storm,' she said, and Sandy smiled. 'What was it you threw in the sea?'

'A penny.'

'Offering to Poseidon?'

'Just felt like it.'

Virginia nodded. She had done the same herself more than once. She looked down. In five minutes, three perhaps, they would cross Ralph's path, if all held their course.

'I—'

She and Sandy both opened their mouths at the same moment.

'I was only going to ask you about Dora.'

'And I was wondering what you thought of her.'

Careful. Though why bother? He'll know what you feel anyway, he always does. It's his reaction that is unpredictable.

'She's—unusual.'

'You mean weird.'

'A bit. But then I hardly know her.'

'But you're right. She is. She's extraordinary.' Sandy's tone was light, but he looked anxious. 'I think I'm in love with her.'

'Think?'

He grinned. 'Not sure what it is.'

'Neither am I. Except it seems to be something we're

all after, doesn't it, and it's not always the deserving who get it.' And, oh Lord, let him have it, she thought in ferocious maternal prayer, may he be loved and not passed over, for he is the best of us all, and will never know it. She glanced back and for just one second of painful animal foreboding could have run up the hill and tipped Dora Phenicule over the cliff.

She must let it go, she knew, this first moment of intimacy for years. Two years, precisely, when the ease between them—that had, perhaps, been in the first place unusual—was lost; quite abruptly, as though in the middle of a conversation Sandy had turned away to the window and never till now looked back.

Any moment the girl would be with them or they would meet Ralph. Still, some things could be said.

'Where did you meet her?'

'The Tate.'

'Oh yes. Art history.' Virginia took a breath. 'She was talking about this paranormal business and Grandpa.'

He frowned. 'I wish she wouldn't. People don't always understand.'

'Do you?'

'I don't think much about it. It's just part of Dora.'

Jackie was running to meet them, ears flipped inside-out by the wind, his barks snatched away.

'It might be better if we didn't bother Grannie with all that—'

Sandy nodded. 'Though I can't tell Dora what to say. And I never know what she's going to say next.'

Then, approaching, Ralph Stephens waved his stick,

and, at the same moment, Dora came down the hill behind him, caught Sandy by the hand and they ran all the way to the bottom, Jackie in ecstasy at their heels.

Riding the south-westerly, Oliver saw them and, through his eyes, so did Humble as she dusted his room, so far as dusting was possible. She picked things up and put them down more heavily than usual. This was too many people by far—she felt as if she had bees in her hair and there would be no peace any more. It wasn't the work she minded—rooms to be opened and beds to be aired—but the presences filling up the air; they made it muddy and confused her. Which was worse, the girl or the dog, she wasn't sure but at least the dog slept in the shed. The girl left more hairs around than the dog did and she'd upset Sir Oliver, you could see. Talk of getting up. Talk of going out. Seen her coming, Humble had, plain on the screen in the middle of *Dallas*, interfering with the picture. No good changing channels or adjusting the set. That night there was the fog, and she'd told Jimminy, her canary: here comes Miss Trouble.

'Susan Humble, you're grumbling, your lips are moving.'

'Oh, we're awake are we?'

Oliver pulled his cardigan around his shoulders with disdain. He was monarchical this morning, lordly.

'I was never asleep. I would like a lamb cutlet, underdone, and a glass of claret.'

'Gallivanting, eh? Those who listen at keyholes get

their ears burned.' Humble carried on, thumping his books into what she considered order, he chaos. 'It's shepherd's pie anyway, with this lot.'

'You are being impertinent.'

She challenged him with those damn bottle-glass spectacles and an alarmingly tight permanent wave, like iron worms.

Oliver looked down, hiding his slyness, then up. Just a quiver of the lip.

'I am a fond and foolish old man. Forgive me, Mrs Humble.'

'Putting it pretty doesn't make it better.'

'You are right, of course. Your simplicity is my illumination, Humble.'

Humble sniffed, would not be placated. She knew who she was and that she had gifts he could do with, not to be mocked. Yet, in a way, she supposed, she felt some love for the old crow, and they had jogged along well enough. They had secrets between them.

She feared that most of all—that the girl had got from him those matters that were private, as if someone had looked into her own cupboards at home, and her workbox, and counted her pins.

Oliver sighed.

'My darling love, my Kitty. Just in time.' Just in time, indeed, he had heard a soft step, tipped the toothglass of Sweet British Sherry into the commode (filthy stuff that Humble woman had brought up from the kitchen when he had specified Harrods' Dry) and arranged his head on the pillow in the attitude of a martyr weary from the rack; rather fine, he thought, from a glance in the mirror opposite. He had longed truthfully for this moment. If only he could squeeze a tear.

'Olly.'

It was Kitty whose eyes pricked. Although, after all, she had enjoyed the journey, it had wearied her, and now there was the disquiet of returning to the island, to the house, the haunted places. Dear Ralph had been kind—as he always was—which might explain why people often failed to notice him, especially if Oliver were around; that was one of life's injustices—in this world Ralph lived alone with a noisy dog while Olly lorded it here with all the pusses for company and everyone at his beck and call. The deserving get short shrift, she supposed, because they never grab the long one. Was she deserving? Kitty could not have said. She had very little idea of herself, which is not to say she was meek.

He had seized her hand and closed his eyes. There was a distinct smell of sherry. Ginny said he had refused the doctor and she really wondered if he were ill at all—but then she seemed distracted herself. Perhaps it was the fuss of coping with a houseful, Kitty couldn't tell; in fact, when she came to think about it, she knew very little about her youngest daughter. Margaret, with her frightful animals and her Shelter was beyond human ken, Pippa sweet, pliant, still a child herself in spite of all those children. But Ginny eluded her in a much

96

more subtle way than Margaret: they could, should, have been close, Kitty felt, yet they were never comfortable. Possibly Ginny had chosen Oliver after the parting? She had brought Lucy once to stay at St Marie-la-Douce but that was years ago when Lucy was a baby, and it had been an awkward, jagged visit. Could she be jealous of the time Sandy spent there? It seemed unlikely. For Ginny's generation possessiveness was a cardinal sin.

Absently, Kitty patted Oliver's hand.

'Well, what's all this then? You know, you really shouldn't send telegrams, upsetting people. I don't believe you're very ill at all.'

I must be strong, Kitty thought, arm myself, not to be ensorcelled. Think of something else, make your own spell. Minette on the warm terrace, investigating the little salamander with fastidious paw, claws in, sniffing the geranium—the only cat she knew who appreciated flowers. Or perhaps she was simply investigating.

Olly had seized her wrist with surprising vigour.

'You have joined them! You too have betrayed me.'

'Oliver, that is absurd, I shall not discuss it. Now, tell me, where is Alcestis? Is she well?'

'Kitty, how could you abandon me? You know what a fool I am without you. I have been lost.'

She decided he was a force-field, it took all her will not to be drawn in. She was breathless. Could he be stealing her oxygen? Such mad thoughts he conjured, but oh, she had loved him, he had consumed her, he had lit a burning brand for her to follow and called her spirit from her flesh.

'You know why I left you.'

Now Oliver was the breathless one, Kitty had winded him. She felt no pride in the fact.

'It's hot in here,' she said. 'Oh, look, isn't that Ginny and the others? Coming down Poet's Walk?' He knew, he had been there with them, riding the gale. 'And who's this!' Kitty opened the window.

'Alcestis.' Oliver's voice was faint. Not faked this time.

'Of course, it must be. How are you, my dear?'

The cat, as it happened, was not at all well. She had stolen the pound of mince from the kitchen dresser, gone out to be sick, and stood now, coat spiked with rain and rage at this invasion of her private chamber. What was worse, she was ignored.

'Kitty? D'you remember the roses in Damascus?'

'Oh yes!'

Memory was a trick she guessed he would use and one she should run from. She knew all about dreams— the good and the bad—and how for the old they could spill into the day until there was hardly any present left. Live in the minute, she said to herself, but it took so little prompting—just a nudge—and there she was, back in the garden among lilies and roses and Olly coming down the path towards her.

As she might when in pain—in childbirth, at the dentist, when rheumatism stabbed and knotted her— Kitty concentrated her mind elsewhere. An apocalyptic cloud she could see from the window, over Cerdic's throne—heavy and bruise-purple against a burst of gold; the peacock sheen (though that of a dusty bird) to Oliver's plum-coloured spread; the slate clock that had been his father's; those might save her, and the chrysanthemums that had been too long stuck (by Humble, she imagined) in a plain pot and smelled of cabbage, rot, change, decay, death.

Briskly she said, 'I'll get those thrown away.' She spoke with one hand on the door. 'If you won't get up, Olly, I think you should have a doctor and a bath.'

Downstairs, Kitty hurried past the kitchen where Humble was banging pots, and in the chilly study helped herself to a very large sherry which she swallowed like medicine, pulling a face. She wondered if there were time to weep, but already that dog of Ralph's was barking in the garden. They must be back.

The various cats stiffened at Jackie's cry.

Since the disappearance of the mince, lunch was tinned ham and tomatoes.

The obvious suspect, Jackie, wagged his tail, and, when scolded, was downhearted; while the true villain lay in the arms of Oliver, her love, and hummed deep in her throat with bliss.

The burst of gold Kitty had observed in the west heralded the kind of English Saturday afternoon described by weathermen as sunny with occasional showers; meaning a continuous downpour would give way every so often to that liquid sun—the finger of God pointing—favoured by Victorian marine painters to represent the last vision of a drowning man as he loses his grip of the raft.

So, of course, everyone went for a walk.

With Humble gone home, Sandy and Dora offered to stay in for Oliver while Virginia went over to Pippa's; she might call at Mag's on the way.

Normally Kitty would have taken her siesta after lunch, the shutters closed, a glass of mineral water with a slice of lemon on her bedside table, and Minette at her feet. Today, in spite of the large sherry before that peculiar ham, she could not settle but prowled the bookshelves—not in the glum study that she still thought of as her father-in-law's, but in what used to be called the sewing-room—small, cosy and, apart from her bedroom, the place in the house she had often chosen to sit. Here were the same faded chintz armchair and the shelf bearing books she must once have loved. Enchanted, she touched their spines. Charles Morgan— how extraordinary; Rose Macaulay, dear Elizabeth Bowen and Rosamond Lehmann. Oh! *Invitation to the Waltz*, what a good old friend. Would they still get on? She could hardly believe not. The novels they wrote nowadays Kitty found sad and often baffling company— many seemed to be warning of something one would prefer not to contemplate. Perhaps since the decay of the Church, the writer had taken on the admonitory role? Kitty smiled at the notion—how that would have enraged her father-in-law!

'Ralph! You made me jump.'

'Jackie and I were going for a walk—if you'd like to come?'

'I would. Yes, very much.' So she would, Kitty realised with surprise. After this morning's upset a walk with sensible Ralph was just what she needed; an *English* walk with boots and brolly. She gave Rosamond Lehmann a parting pat—'After tea, my dear.'

Mag opened the door and Virginia was swallowed by dogs.

'Down chaps! Good timing—Pippa's here.'

Pippa emerged, clutching one of her brood.

'Looking for a puppy for Saul.'

'You came to the right place.' Virginia hugged Pippa. Mag, one did not hug. 'Sam's got one for Lucy. I think it's a mistake.'

Mag caught this. 'Doggies in London? Not fair. Can't give the boys a run.'

'Well, there is the heath.'

'I thought Saul ought to have one because of the baby.' Pippa seemed to find it necessary to explain. 'I mean, then he'd have his own, so to speak.'

'Baby?'

'Puppy.'

Are we going to talk about dogs forever, Virginia wondered? She took off her soaking headscarf and looked for somewhere to sit. Once this had been a bungalow to which Mag had attached a dog sanctuary. Now it was a kennel in which Mag camped. People brought her strays. She went looking for them. There had been threats that she might be charged with causing a nuisance—something to do with sheep—but Mag seemed to ride all troubles. Locally, she was a figure of fun and Virginia wondered how much this hurt her sister, or if Mag might be one of those blessed beings so sure of her purpose nothing touched her. One shouldn't laugh at Mag—she might even be happy.

Mag made thick brown tea. Saul (reluctant) was introduced to a number of squirming puppies. Virginia smiled, sat back, let her eyes close and felt the sun on her face. From here, Dora's fantasies seemed mercifully absurd. She opened her eyes. Mag had jammed two wild daisies in a milk bottle on the windowsill. Saul had begun to bawl and the dogs to bark.

Pippa's eyes filled with sympathetic tears: for Saul, for the dogs, for everyone.

'Mag, I think maybe not today, if that's all right. It was sweet of you. But I can't leave Eric with the brood much longer. Are you coming, Ginny?'

'If you can give me a lift.'

'Oh dear,' Pippa said in the estate van, 'd'you think she was hurt?'

'Shouldn't think so.'

'Come back for tea. Proper tea, I mean.'

'Fine.'

'You must be worn out with that lot. I'll come and see Mother tomorrow or have her over.'

Virginia nodded. What was the point in telling Pippa? She'd only take it seriously and then worry. What Virginia needed was someone to laugh, to blow away the crazy speculations Dora's confession had aroused. Virginia needed sense, reason, humour, Sam.

In their orchard, Pippa's Eric was picking apples with one of those long-handled gadgets to reach the high ones. He smiled and waved. Saul, let out of the van, ran towards his father. Life can be very simple, thought Virginia—as simple as that. Sentiment, of course, but at Pippa's—drinking tea from blue mugs, listening as sturdy Eric explained the reliability of Bramleys, the waywardness of Cox's—she enjoyed the sensation of having wandered into some prelapsarian garden. She knew better: scratch the surface and lo! there lies coiled the serpent; but for the moment she relished the illusion of peace and innocence. Home again, Saul was playing happily, Pippa peaceful as a good woman in a Dutch painting. In herself, Virginia knew, there was something sharp, abrasive, but here it dozed, along with malice and rage and passion and fear.

'I do love it here,' Virginia said. She picked up the newspaper. In the last few days she had quite forgotten there was a world outside—not that the local paper had much to say about that. There had been a rabies scare on the island, a production of *The Pirates of Penzance* and an air-sea rescue. Royalty had opened something.

'Lord!' she folded back the paper. 'Have you seen this? They're selling Cerdic's throne!'

On the front at the Bar Kitty was glad that she and Ralph had decided to drive here instead of walking. It was quite a relief to find one's tramping days were over.

The sea was breaking on the pier. Jackie was making a one-dog attempt to clear the beach of seagulls. Ralph was breathing in and out.

'Good air. Better than Sussex.'

'Lovely,' Kitty panted. She might have been made of twigs. A gull could have snatched her up and carried her off. A gust flung her against Ralph and Kitty rather liked being steadied. A rock without complications, she thought—how nice, and what folly to imagine even for a moment that someone had parted those racing clouds like curtains, and peered out.

Sandy and Dora were looking after Oliver. They were on the sofa in the sewing-room, watching wrestling on television.

'Like that, you see,' said Dora, 'then you can't move.' For a slim girl, she was astonishingly strong.

'Be careful. You might break something.' Sandy groaned. 'But don't stop.'

'Is that a double Burton?'

'Half Nelson. No, I don't think so. This is impossible. Are you double-jointed?'

'Now your turn.'

Kicking off his jeans, already round his ankles, Sandy whooped and pounced. 'I love you!'

From somewhere between the centre lampshade and the ceiling Dora smiled down upon their tangled limbs.

Bliss.

PART TWO

8

'*P*lease don't tell Grandfather about the throne.'
'He knows already.'
'How did he get hold of the paper?'
'He didn't. Dora told him.'
Virginia slammed down a plate.
'I could shake her.'
'You know Grandfather. He'd have found out anyway.'
Virginia had to agree with Sandy. In any case, it was the world that needed protecting from Oliver, she thought sometimes. When they were children someone—it must have been Humble—told them that it was Oliver who made the thunder and lightning. Possibly this was meant to be reassuring, but it made Pippa scream in the night. One could see Pippa's point—if he conjured it then surely he could stop it too? Certainly ever since, even into sceptical adulthood, Virginia had retained the fantasy of Oliver's wizardry; not that he could do magic, exactly (as all

the children had believed who saw his Christmas con-
juring)——more that he was an impresario of life.
He manipulated people, she had known that for as
long as she could remember. More recently, she had
grasped that he stage-managed events. Thus, she suspected, he had brought them all to the island, though
with what in mind probably even he could not have
said.

And now there was this crazy business——according
to Flora-Dora. Virginia felt she must be mad herself to
give it any credence at all. And yet.

Virginia gave up at the sink and sat slumped at
the kitchen table. She reached in the pocket of her
smock. O K, Sam, I'm smoking again. Well, come and
stop me then. Dammit, no matches. She raked her
hands through her hair, got up, opened a couple
of drawers, riffled through and slammed them shut,
found the matches on the dresser shelf and sat down
again.

Sandy was regarding her warily. There was something
wild about his mother. Perhaps there always had been
and he had never noticed? Come to think of it, he'd
never looked. You didn't, did you, your own parents?
When he had dropped out of college she hadn't seemed
angry——nor had his father; in a way, he wished they had
been angry, but all they said was: oh well, your own life.
A shrug when a scene would have been natural. Relieved
though he was, he had found this oddly hurtful. Incon-
venient too——a drama would have made it easier to
leave.

110

Now, regarding her, he wondered if Virginia might be afraid of her own rage? It was a momentary intuition, then his thoughts turned again to Dora. Just lately, they hardly ever left her.

Sitting in the window-seat with a book in her lap, Dora exclaimed, 'But it's all here!'

'All what?' Oliver grunted. In his mind he was framing a letter to the National Trust. Or should it be the Minister for the Environment? Ralph might know. He'd always been a nuts-and-bolts man. Good old friend. Pity about that yapping beast—it was making the puss-cats nervy. Sir! The wanton sale of our national heritage . . .

'Here! In your Plato. How they were all born again! And they could choose and then they forgot, except one—like you, I suppose. How funny—Orpheus wanted to be a swan to get away from women and a swan chose to be a man. No one wanted to come back as they had been, even the heroes. That's sad. But it's beautiful. Listen. "At last they encamped at evening by the river of Forgetfulness, whose water no pitcher may hold. All had to drink a certain measure of this water, but those who were not preserved by wisdom drank more than the measure. Each as he drank it forgot everything. Then they went to sleep, and it was midnight; there was thunder and an earthquake, and at once they were carried up from thence along different ways to their birth, shooting like stars." That's lovely. I

111

wish I could remember. What would you choose if you could?'

'Oblivion.' Oliver pulled down the corners of his mouth. Dora regarded him sternly. Today she wore her hair in two coils, like earphones; the effect—that of a striking Portia—was only slightly diminished by the fact that one chestnut loop was planted lower than the other.

'Nonsense. You know you're dying of curiosity. Sorry! But you know what I mean.'

'Perhaps.' She was right, of course: however much he clung to this life, there was always that itch of anticipation—what next?

'How much *do* you remember?'

Oliver blew his nose. No one had ever talked to him like this preposterous child. Uneasily he wondered if he, who had always been the motivator, had met his match.

'Not everything, but then, of course, one has no idea what everything would amount to. Much slips through the net, no doubt. The rest is occasionally very clear, mostly like a dream—distant voices, shapes half-formed.' He closed his eyes. Beneath his lids the faces seethed, pressed for recognition. Bells tolled, not of this world, heard through seas of time. Wax in the ears.

'You have known me before. Tell me.'

'I don't remember. Scraps. Words. *Hic incipit vita.*'

'When was that?' Dora was kneeling by the bed now, her hand touching his.

112

'A child was born. I was drunk.'
'You loved me?'
He shook his head. Tired. Too much.

Later, she brought up his tea.

'It's dark so early now. I'll turn on the lights.' Before drawing the curtains, Dora paused. 'There's a terrific moon—you can see Poet's Walk. What are you doing about the throne? Are you going to get up?'

Walking home, Susan Humble observed the twin moons. The actual planet, boiling amber for harvest, a giant eye on the horizon, very close—and the other, smaller glow from Oliver's window, where a figure was pulling the curtains. She could guess who that was, been up there half the day, Miss Baggage and Trollop; exciting the old man and then they'd all pay for it.

Last night the Virgin Mary had appeared in the *Rover's Return*—real as Len Fairclough or Annie Walker—and advised her to give notice. She wore blue, of course, and was quite a bit older than Humble had imagined, though when you came to think about it that was to be expected. It wasn't as if she stopped getting older once He was born. She was very nice to talk to, and after she had gone Humble felt happy—almost as she had when she was a child and woke up on a summer morning in the holidays, to a clear sky.

It was marvellous what you could see if you looked, if you had eyes to see.

Sam came over with Lucy. He would leave her for half-term and stay the weekend himself. Virginia met them at the Hovercraft terminal, hugged Lucy and found herself—she who never cried—weeping in Sam's arms.

'Really, it's all right, I'm happy. I'm happy now, it's better.'

'Apparently.' He kissed her again before he took the wheel. 'Sure?'

She nodded. The moment she had seen him under the lamp she had felt him restored to her; or each, rather, to their marriage—the organism to which both were subservient. How strange, how wonderful, this tissue of years and habit, concern and battle, taste of skin—marriage. Lucy watched from the back seat with large eyes. Virginia squeezed her hand. 'Lulu.'

There was a queue. Waiting under the sodium lights, Virginia picked up the paper Sam had brought from the mainland. Lucy was chattering about the puppy. *Reagan steps up nuclear arms.* 'Oh, God.'

'Did you say something?'

Virginia shook her head. She suddenly realised, how strange, this is something we, our friends, never talk about. The small wars, yes, but the probability of extinction is not polite. She shivered, touched Sam's sleeve.

'Well, what about this puppy?'

'What a moon. It seems threatening, like the sun by night.' Virginia pulled the curtains and joined Sam in the single bed. The house was stuffed to bursting. She had put Lucy on the sofa, and wondered vaguely if it mattered that the child would see her brother was sharing his bed. No choice anyway. Ralph Stephens seemed disinclined to leave even though he had seen very little of Oliver. 'I've missed you.'

'Mmn.'

'You know I've always loved it here—the island, everything. But this time it seems different. I can't explain. I expect I'm just tired.'

'Come back with us.'

'If I could. But Mother can't run the house and Humble would give notice. Oh, Sam.' She drew his head to her breast.

'Can I come in?'

'Yes please.'

A brilliant frost. Oliver's letter to *The Times* appeared in the same issue as the advertisement for the sale of Cerdic's throne. Frost so early was unusual on the island. It blackened the dahlias and for a transitory shining moment gave the illusion of an earth re-created and restored to purity. The night before, a spokesman for the Society for the Preservation of Rural England had appeared on *Nationwide* with representatives of the Church Commissioners—who were selling—and the National Trust—who couldn't afford to buy. Oliver shouted for the television to be turned off, took a swig from the Milpar bottle and called for books, files, paper, pen, cutting off the rest of Sue Lawley (to whom, since the traitorous disappearance of Anna Ford, he had transferred his affections).

By the time Virginia brought in his hot milk, he was too bright-eyed, querulous, the papers spilling from the bed. When she had gone he blew on the milk to cool it, put it down for Alcestis and lay back, exhausted. What a fool! He, who had been with old England so long he should be weary of her, fretting at the disposal of a lump of granite of dubious heritage. All those lives! Nothing learned! He was as bad as those fools gaping already for Halley's comet; and he'd seen that madness often enough—since the spring of 1066 and no doubt before that if he could remember. Better forgotten, all the rubbish of history, public and private. Or so he felt tonight; and yet he brooded on Cerdic's throne. Humble, tranced, had seen in her vision the Saxon set there on the throne watching for the Danes. Almost as good a perch as Xerxes above the straits of Salamis (and about as propitious).

Fumbling impatiently among his papers, Oliver found the file at last—under the bed, the territory private to him and Humble.

I see him looking for the long ships . . . they will burn his castle and cast him from his stone and others with him.

Did Humble in her vision mean this literally? That Cerdic was flung from the cliff or leapt at the last moment with those who remained to him? The Saxon's end had always been in doubt. Most theories had been discredited or unproven and folklore thrived on mystery: hence the stone was invested with the muddle of legend, which frequently obfuscated more than it illumined.

Oliver dropped the file back under the bed. Time for a pee. Not that he'd sleep a wink tonight. He tried gently to push, then to unclaw Alcestis from the eiderdown, but with a look of amber reproach, she refused to budge. Very nervy she'd been the last few days and Oliver knew why. Damn dog.

Kitty could not remember when she had last walked before breakfast. She was finding it remarkably pleasant, stepping out with her stick beside Ralph, Jackie quiet and well-behaved, off about his own affairs in the hedgerows twenty yards ahead.

'The frost is so lovely. A pity it kills.'

Ralph nodded. 'It'll be worse in Sussex—polish off my last roses.'

The abbey bell called. The sky was a clear, dry blue. As though signalled by the bell, a pigeon rose from the black conifers set at the boundary of the abbey grounds.

'Are you happy, Ralph? In Sussex, I mean?'

Ralph whacked the dead head off a nettle.

117

'I thought I was.'

'Thought?'

Ralph stopped as though called to halt.

'I'm in love with you, Kitty. I always have been. Don't answer me. Don't say anything.'

Kitty gasped. 'But Ralph—'

'I shouldn't speak, I know. Loyalty to Oliver. But before I leave the island I'll ask you to come with me, to marry me, whatever you choose. If not to marry me, then to live with me; if not to live with me, then to see me. If not that, to write; at least to think of me.'

In the brief moment of Ralph's speaking, as a second pigeon rose close to them, with a clatter of wings, and flew to join the first, Kitty remembered so much, as though door after door had been flung open and she could look back down the long avenue of her life, no longer dark: the touch of Ralph's hand in Venice (pigeons there too, but all around) and further back still, a dance, the dunes outside the Spitview Hotel, a kiss. That had been the dancing time when—now she could admit it to herself—she had suspected Olly of having an affair with Ralph's Angela. But perhaps this had been the secret, after all. Well.

And the strange thing was that Kitty was neither shocked nor alarmed. She could have given no response, even if Ralph had asked for it, yet she was not as surprised as she should have been. Had she known all the time, she wondered? Are there truths we seal away from ourselves, then the wax is broken and we are not amazed?

Certainly since his declaration Kitty saw Ralph differently, herself too. He, oddly, seemed more real— as though she had never looked at him properly before. Could she see him as the loved one? At this moment anything appeared possible. It was all rather thrilling. For so long the image she had had of herself was that of an old woman, someone to whom nothing would ever happen except death. When she allowed herself to think ahead, all she could envisage was going into the darkness. Might there, after all, be something yet to come?

Only a week ago Kitty would have regarded any such thinking as wild and disturbing, not to be entertained. The idea of change would have been alarming, unthinkable. But she had taken the first step and her life had altered.

'Ralph, dear.' She took his arm as they turned to walk back down the hill.

'I haven't shocked you?'

'Oh no. Not a bit. But I'll have to think.'

'Of course.'

Kitty smiled.

'Look—the frost has gone.'

So it had, and with the warming sun the village gardens gave off breaths of mist. Kitty and Ralph did not notice Alcestis curled in a sun-trap by the Post Office wall, screened by Michaelmas daisies, but the cat saw them.

After breakfast Kitty and Ralph went off in Ralph's car and would be gone, they said, until tea-time.

'Well, that's two out of the way,' Virginia said. 'Honestly, Mrs Humble, it was marvellous of you to come in, but there's no need to spoil your weekend.'

Humble looked doubtful, demurred, but at last she had gone. Virginia watched her small resolute figure— tied up at the waist like a neat parcel—until Humble reached the gate and paused to look back and up. At Oliver's window, Virginia assumed.

'She really does get odder and odder.' Virginia poured herself another coffee, topped up Sam's mug and joined him at the table, *The Times* open between them. She could see, upside-down, the picture of Cerdic's throne on the property page. 'Or perhaps just older? I've never thought about her age—I can't remember her being young, she just seems always to have been here. Thank heaven. But she's jealous. I think she wants Father to herself. It's a bit sad. A couple of hundred years ago she'd have been one for the ducking-stool.'

She peered over Sam's shoulder at the advertisement. '"Nation's heritage with great potential for leisure trade." Really! For once I almost agree with Father, though I wish he hadn't got involved. What do you make of his letter?'

Sam tipped back his chair. The sun streamed onto his face and he half-closed his lids. He needed a shave. His black hair, greying, curled tightly, his neck was strongly planted, corded with muscle. He's a centaur, Virginia thought—Sagittarian horse-man. He's been working too hard, always does.

Sam said, 'He's making a moral issue of it. The wrong approach.'

'But isn't it? Public loos on Poet's Walk? Tea and toilets. Grotty souvenirs? Saxon tea-towels.'

'You're being patronising.'

Virginia smiled. She could imagine that Sam would have said the same twenty years ago, but had the sense not to remind him. The more affluent he became, the more he was a Man of the People—provided he didn't have to live with them. Since he didn't care for the island, the present issue was a matter of indifference to him.

'But history,' she said. 'They haven't even excavated there.'

'What d'you expect to find? Cerdic's crown and wellies?'

'Blast you. Cerdic was said to have had Celtic blood too, you know. I can't think why you're being so obstinate. It could be a rich archaeological site.'

Sam followed her into the garden. They stood in the deep wet grass. By next spring the neglected beds would have returned to nature. Decay, Virginia thought. Mutability. Renewal? She had doubts of that.

'Ginny, love, what's up?'

She shook her head.

'Oliver?'

'Maybe. Myself too. That is, Father's been having fantasies—according to Sandy's girl—and I can't quite laugh at them. It's as though I'd been caught up somehow. You know what he's like. And this place.'

They were wading in leaves now, his hand on her shoulder. She couldn't talk, she couldn't tell him, nor could she go home.

At that moment, stirring the damp leaves with her foot, Virginia understood that she did not wish to leave, even if she could. Acknowledging this to herself, she felt calmer. They walked on up to the shack that had once been the summerhouse. Now the door was gone and the half-wild garden invaded—the floor was adrift with leaves, a croquet mallet and child's cricket bat slept in dust and webs; there was even evidence that a swallow had nested here—perhaps only just left. Sam sat on the step. Virginia brushed leaves from the deckchair and tested the canvas.

'This was one of the places Pippa and I played house. We didn't let Mag in. Poor Mag. Yet she seems happy enough. It's impertinent, isn't it, to judge other people's state of mind by their circumstances?' She looked out over the garden to the sea where a few late yachts— stunned moths clinging to a cold window-pane—lay becalmed; and further to the mainland. People lived there, teemed, yet the only evidences of habitation were a few fingers of smoke pointing to the sky, and the ferry emerging from the mouth of the harbour. When they were small, the mainland had been a wonderful place: America, Greenland, Africa, the matter of dreams.

'You know, sometimes I think of England like Father —a petulant old man who won't get up, living in the past. A tyrant. Up to all kinds of tricks, making impossible demands.'

122

Sam turned his face to her and Virginia kissed him softly on the lips.

'So do you understand why I must stay?'

'No, but I'll put up with it.'

They sat on.

'Have you talked to Sandy yet?' she said.

'What's the point? He won't talk to me. I don't know why. Some time I suppose I said the wrong thing or failed to say the right thing.'

'I feel a bit like that.'

'God save us from our children.'

Virginia laughed. She stood, pulling Sam to his feet. On a surge of irrational well-being, she felt life to be glorious in this garden of golden, bounteous decay. She called to Lucy—playing with a cat on the lower lawn— 'Come on! Let's rake the leaves.'

On the leeward side of the throne it was sheltered enough for Sandy and Dora to eat their picnic. Sandy exclaimed.

'Whatever did you put in the sandwiches?'

Dora reflected.

'I didn't like to take anything proper your mother might miss. Some bacon from the breakfast plates, apricot marmalade and half a tin of tuna fish I found in the fridge. It looked rather old, as though it had been forgotten.'

'That was for the cats! Christ. Dora.' Sandy groaned and flung his lunch to the gulls. The smaller black-caps were shy but the big yellow-eyed brutes came close enough to snatch the crusts from his hand. Their wing-span never ceased to astonish him, nor their grace in the air—the intricacy of their weaving and their resting and curving and soaring and dipping; then the moment they touched earth, their clumsy ugliness.

Dora regarded him sternly.

'You're sulking.' She pondered. 'You're not *jealous*, are you?' Sandy flung the last lump of bread.

'Of course I am.'

'But that's crazy.'

'You spend more time with him than you do with me.'

'Yes, I expect you're right. I'm sorry.'

Sandy pulled up a tuft of grass.

'Why did he want us all here, anyway?'

'To see what would happen?'

'What do you talk about?'

'Anything. Everything.' She shrugged. 'I think we met in another life. You remember, at the Tate? Jeanne Hébuterne?'

It took Sandy a moment to grasp what she meant.

'You're not saying you were grandfather's mistress in another life?'

She chose her words. 'We seem to recognise each other.'

Sandy got to his feet and stamped around the stone.

'That's crazy!'

'No, it happens all the time. Haven't you ever seen anyone you thought you knew, yet you couldn't have met them before? Or arrived somewhere new and felt you'd been there before?'

124

He sat down again, back to the stone, but stiff.

'That's just déjà-vu—something to do with the sub-conscious.'

'Sandy. Please. You've always believed me before.' Dora put her face to his and wrapped her blanket-cloak around his shoulders. 'Stay with me. It won't be long.'

With a sound between a sob and a groan, Sandy allowed himself to be entirely enveloped in Dora's blanket. Inside Dora—that was the only place to be.

This heaven-sent day, Humble was pottering in her small garden. Best to keep busy, not to brood about the goings-on up there. A person has her own life. Not to be puffed up and proud, but to know who you are: Susan Humble, nothing more nor less. That was enough.

Crisp weather in autumn and, with sunshine, there is beauty in a cabbage, especially the Savoys. As Humble worked between the rows on her kneeling mat, with her dibber and her yellow gardening gloves, she had the feeling of someone helping, tidying behind her. She caught just a glimpse of a blue sleeve.

9

The island hummed. The Electricity Board denied responsibility. It was a sound that drove dogs to howl in the night, when it could be most distinctly heard.

Though distinct it never was: more a mumbling of the senses, a tinnitus of the ears and the wits that drove the more sensitive to earplugs and sleeping pills. Others— the cranks, the seekers-after-truth, the UFO brigade, the lost in the world, the children and the merely curious—were drawn to the western point of the island, up Poet's Walk to Cerdic's throne.

Some claimed to receive a slight electric shock on touching the stone; others that it was radioactive.

So far they came only in small numbers, for this was not yet national news; besides, it was winter, out of season, and Poet's Walk was a steep climb.

Oliver saw them from his turret lavatory. They were like pilgrims. They sought magic.

At night, Mag was woken by the ululation of her hounds. She let them out but they refused to go. The seventh night she resorted to rum in their drinking water and the rest of the bottle for herself.

Pippa's children—especially the youngest—seemed to welcome this weird night music; she herself put cotton wool in her ears and in bed curled closer to Eric.

The battle on *The Times* letter page continued. In Oliver's train had come the environmentalists, the academics, the politicians and the professional letter writers. Oliver retired for the moment from the hustle, consulted his notes and files and books, and cracked his knuckles. Secretly, he stepped up his night-time exercise regime. Preparing for what, though, he could not have said. They were nervous downstairs, he knew that.

At other times he was seized by such weariness the only person he could bear in the room was Dora. Then he would send her too away and, propped on his pillows, watch the teasing thumb of granite on the headland shift in the mist, Protean, a throne, a stone, a shrine, a tomb. He shivered and pulled up the eiderdown, reached for the comfort of Alcestis's warm fur.

The rain fell. Oliver's day-dreams were bad and as he tossed Kitty was aware of her returning arthritis; she pined for her warm mountainside and was irritated by the way Ralph ate his boiled eggs—there was something military about the precision with which he decapitated the poor things. And how she could ever have entertained the idea of that dog! Of actually living with it! She was a traitor to Minette.

Sandy and Dora quarrelled and this time did not entirely make up. She went for a walk alone, was gone all day, and he thought she had fallen down a cliff as she had when they first arrived. By the time she got back he was looking for her in the dark and the fog. They slept what was left of the night back to back. In the morning Dora had a cold. Sandy took his social security money from the tobacco tin he hid inside his sleeping bag and went to London, to Gloria and Gregory's. The rain was even worse in London, where it seemed not a natural element, but a punishment.

Dora knitted and sneezed. Humble slammed the pots and broke the last of the crystal wine glasses, that had been the old Rector's. It was the hum, she said.

Hum.

Ralph Stephens straightened his tie and checked his moustache. He glanced round his room—all ship-shape. Every morning he made his own bed—hospital corners —and reviewed the troops; shaving equipment to attention on the glass shelf above the washbasin, bedside book in place, likewise pyjama case, and dressing-gown on hanger behind the door.

Lately, not for the first time, his precision irked him. A defensive posture developed first at public school and through an unhappy marriage, it had become impossible to throw off; now, when he most needed abandon, he could not call upon it. Kitty judged him decent but dull, he suspected: probably all the more after the clumsiness of his declaration.

He brushed his walking shoes to go out in the downpour. Passing the sewing-room he caught a glimpse of Kitty by the gas fire and sighed. There was no doubt she had cooled, and he could hardly stay much longer in Oliver's house, trying to steal his wife. No better than a burglar! Move to the pub? Build him a willow cabin at her gate?

'No good, Jackie old boy,' Ralph said to his dog as they set off down the hill, 'I'm a passionate pilgrim in disguise.'

'Like wax in the ears,' said Kitty, 'a humming noise.'

'It's been in the papers.' Virginia had meant to let down the hem of Lucy's winter school skirt but sherry seemed a good idea. Whisky would have been better but when she went to get the last bottle from the larder she found it nearly empty. Certainly not Ralph Stephens, not his style. Sandy didn't like whisky and Flora-Dora Phenicule seemed to be everything but a toper. Virginia poured a large sherry and the same for her mother. Then they had another. It was the first time the two women had been truly alone since Kitty arrived.

Virginia said, 'I think someone's been smuggling whisky up to Father. Must be Humble.'

'It doesn't seem so bad in the rain.' Kitty put down the *Daily Telegraph* crossword. Perhaps it was the sherry, but Ginny seemed less intimidating today.

'What?'

'The hum.'

'Ah. Yes.'

'Ralph has just taken that dog out. Or the other way round.' Kitty wondered how Ginny would react if she were to tell her of Ralph's proposal. For a second she had a mad urge to confide.

Virginia walked around the room, glass in hand, shaking a cushion, picking up a magazine and putting it down. She stopped at the window. Rain clouds tore across the sky, with mad glints of green pursuivant. It was a witch's brew of a day. Wind snatched up the gale-torn twigs—one as large as a branch—and flung them across the lawn. Go on! Virginia wanted to cry— blow away the island, England, the whole bloody place! It's only rags and tatters, a puff would do it. Glancing at her mother she thought, how strange to be that generation, to have lived from the certainty of Empire to the probability of the end of the world. Things have got worse lately, in ways I cannot define. Not merely wars and the talk of war but a general unease, a small daily terror. Give us this day our daily bread.

She laid her cheek against the cool, washed pane, and took a deep breath.

'I'm worried about Father.'

'I really don't think you need, dear.'

Why shouldn't Kitty share the problem?

'He's got some cranky idea about reincarnation. And other things.'

'Yes, I know.'

Virginia turned. Kitty sat calmly in the nursing chair, one-eared Priam on her lap in an ecstasy of purrs as she gently scratched his throat.

'You know?'

'That your father lived before, yes. That's why I left him in the end. So many other women, you see, and some he remembered particularly. We did love each other, but he loved them too.'

Virginia sat down.

'And you believed that?'

Kitty nodded. 'I do see now how dreadful it must have been for him. After a while it must be difficult to have ordinary feelings.' She paused for thought. 'On the other hand, normal rules can't be applied to Olly, can they? I believe, you see, that there are powers in the world and your father is one of them. One has to make allowances.'

'Powers?' Virginia gaped—not so much at the substance of Kitty's remark but that Kitty should have made it.

'Don't you think? It's something I feel, but I'm not very clever at explaining. I don't mean good or evil—just forces, so to speak. I suppose there's a word for it.'

'Psychic energy?'

'I expect that's right. Something like electricity perhaps. A few, for better or worse, can plug in and that affects us all—like those power surges when the lights are very bright, that upset the television.' I'm talking too much, Kitty thought, it must be the sherry; but she went on. 'I think sometimes that makes more sense than God, don't you?'

Virginia had got her breath back.

'Or perhaps it is what we call God? Something indifferent, simply there—like the hum.'

'Of course!' Kitty was pleased. She knew she would regret the sherry later but it had been so nice to have a good talk for a change. Especially with Virginia. After all, might it not be too late to make friends with her daughter?

She would stay a little longer, in spite of the weather. Tomorrow there might be a letter—Britt had promised to write about Minette. Certainly too much sherry. Kitty felt silly as a schoolgirl. She leaned confidingly towards Virginia.

'I'm not sure we should be talking like this. Don't you feel sometimes that he's *listening*?'

'God?'

'No. Your father.'

Virginia laughed. 'I wouldn't be surprised. From what Flora-Dora says, he could be up there on the ceiling now.'

'Now I didn't know that!'

'Oh yes—it's called out-of-body experience or something.'

'Well, that explains! On the aeroplane—I could have sworn I saw him looking in. So he really was?'

132

'Probably.'

'I think people who eavesdrop get their ears burned!' said Kitty in a clear voice, quite flushed with daring.

There was Humble. She had heard the giggling and smelled the sherry.

'Mashed?' she said, as it might have been Damned!

Hum.

Dora sneezed, wiped her nose on tissues she kept in a marsupial pouch in her over-garment, and picked up a stitch—her tongue sticking out. Oliver flinched; anyone else diseased would have been banned from his room. Why he let the girl in, he couldn't think.

'Who was this Cerdic anyway?'

In this weather, half the gang of cats were in the room—three, including Alcestis, on the bed, the rest at Dora's feet before the fire.

'I mean, what did he do?'

Oliver rubbed Alcestis's ruff up the wrong way; she swore and batted his face with her paw—claws sheathed.

'Some doubt if he existed at all. I don't. He was a *Bretwalda*. That is, he held what Bede calls the *imperium*— an Anglo-Saxon kingship that conceived of Britain as a whole, that kept alive the idea of Britain. His name is British. He was old England more truly than that beggar, Arthur. Arthur smashed, the house of Cerdic healed and built.'

133

'What about this magic?'

'Magic?' Oliver sat up, scattering cats. 'Who's been talking about magic?' There were two high, bright spots of colour on his cheeks.

'Someone. Sandy. I don't know. You know—that when the Danes came he didn't really die but flew away or something?'

Oliver grumbled. He pulled the eiderdown up to his chin. 'Unhistorical.'

Dora shrugged. 'I don't see all this history matters. But the magic was all right.'

'All that is recorded is that the Danes took the island and burned Cerdic's castle.'

He eyed Dora warily. She blew her nose, long to begin with and now pink-tipped.

'Then what's the fuss about? And the hum? And why are you so bothered about the throne being sold?'

'You are a tiresome child. You're tiring me.'

Triumphantly, Dora increased a stitch: where there had been two, lo, now there were three.

'You're planning something, aren't you?'

'As it happens, I am,' Oliver announced. 'I intend to get up.'

For once, Sandy found no solace in London. He had no heart even for Gloria and Gregory's and the burrows of Balham, for he had been happy here with Dora. She was not there, nor was she in the gallery where in dull pain he revisited the Modiglianis. She was not in the cold at night when he slept, knees drawn up to chin and the sleeping-bag string drawn tight. London was dark. London exploded with the seasonal IRA festivities. London put Gloria's son, Derek-Mohammed, on probation for not being somewhere else when a policeman ran into a brick. London was not a place to hide. London was not Dora.

On the island, rumours flew as mad as the windy rooks that cawed in winter and were flung in tatters across the sky.

Cerdic's throne and the surrounding ten acres had been sold by the Church Commissioners to a holiday-camp chain.

The National Trust had put in a bid.

The National Trust had not put in a bid.

An American oil-baron was planning to dig up the stone, ship it and re-erect it in Texas.

The Minister for the Environment was troubled on television, but on the other hand, Sue, there was only so much in the er-nation's purse and the task of justly apportioning the er-national cake was troubling. Moreover, a survey had shown, what is more, that the limestone cliffs were er-crumbling. The still-leonine mane flung back, a flash of his good capping job. Frankly, Sue, one wouldn't let one's family picnic there.

'I suppose that's probably true—the last bit, anyway,' Virginia said. 'The cliffs have been unsafe for years.'

She was standing in the doorway of the sewing-room.

135

Supper was on and Kitty had called her to see *Nationwide*. Dora was curled in what appeared to Virginia to be coils, on the sofa.

'What about the throne then?'

'That's granite. Either an outcrop or imported. I mean, for some purpose—if not for ritual, then perhaps astronomy, sun-sightings. In that case, it would be much older than Cerdic.'

Dora widened her eyes and blew her nose. She had passed the sneezing stage and was well into the runny. She had stopped up the downstairs loo with Virginia's Boutique tissues.

'No wonder it's hubbing,' she said.

'Up?'

'That's what he says.' Virginia and Kitty sat over their morning coffee in the kitchen. Humble, peeling potatoes at the sink, presented an implacable back. Once or twice lately, Virginia thought she had caught her talking to herself. The last in the series of gales had passed, and Ralph was out in the garden, raking and burning leaves in the sunlight. Jackie kept him company, trotting beside the barrow from lawn to bonfire and back—every so often running off on a game of his own after birds, flying leaves, chimeras—but always returning. In boots and leather-patched jacket, Ralph worked steadily, to a regular private rhythm: so many paces to the bonfire, so many sweeps with the rake, so many steps back to the heap. He would pause occasionally—once to study a miraculously unfrosted rose, once to chat to Jackie and stand for a moment, unlit pipe between his teeth, looking around. Given long enough, Virginia felt sure, he would make out the lines and plantings of the buried, once-beautiful garden, and bring it to life again, with love.

She smiled.

'He's a nice man, isn't he—Ralph.'

He wants to run away with me, Kitty smiled to herself, to love me wildly beyond reason. Now the sun had lifted her mood, to contemplate was delicious—as daring almost as the act itself. But to go? What if she were to say now, to Ginny, I am running away with Ralph; by such a wicked act, spinning for ever out of Olly's orbit. Silly old woman. Too late and nothing to give but the rigidly woven habits of solitude.

Still, she had come this far and she had never expected. Well.

And now Olly not dying but getting up.

Virginia lit a cigarette. The curl of blue smoke in the sunlight. Ralph's bonfire, going nicely now; Virginia liked this autumnal ritual, the illusion of man in control of a domestic and necessary burning, tidying up his earth.

'It was Dora who told me about Father. She seems to be his official spokesman. It's just as well, of course— that he's getting up, I mean. D'you think Dora's behind it?'

'No one makes your father do anything.'

'I wonder what he's up to. Perhaps one shouldn't always assume that he has some motive, but I do.'

Kitty nodded calmly. 'Oh, yes, he generally has.' She *was* enjoying herself; Ralph's flattering attentions, this new ease with Ginny, and, not least, her growing resolution not to be intimidated by Olly. She almost unnerved herself with her own bravado and wondered how long it would last.

'Have you noticed,' she said, 'the hum's louder today.'

Up, thought Humble—and what good will come of that? Her friend, the Virgin Mary, had recommended notice. He had been her friend, too, the daft old fellow —Sukie's only friend—and now it was all altered. He wouldn't even need her for the whisky any more.

All the resolutions she had made failed, for the moment, to sustain her. Only the soft voice in her ear gave her the courage to climb the stairs and knock on Oliver's door.

'Well, I hope Sandy turns up by Sunday lunch,' Virginia said. 'My father never wants people until they're not there; if Sandy isn't, he'll notice. I don't suppose you know where he might be? In London, I suppose.'

Looking for Dora, Virginia had finally come upon her in the summerhouse, nesting with the cats in a deckchair in a puddle of thin sunlight. She was under an eiderdown of feline hot-water bottles.

'I expect so,' said Dora, sneezed and closed her eyes.

I could shake her, Virginia thought, clenching her

hands. I could hit her with a croquet mallet, very hard, on the side of the head. I could pick up those cats by their scruffs and throw them at her.

'If I were you, I shouldn't stay there too long. You might get pneumonia.' Fat chance.

'Oh, there you are.' Kitty was looking at the telephone as though it might blow up in her face. 'Someone wanting to interview Olly. I said I thought not but I'm afraid they'll be back. It'll be about the stone, I suppose.'

'Father, what have you done to Humble?'

'I have done nothing. It is what she has done to me.'

'To us, you mean. She's given notice.'

He waved his hand limply. Virginia thought: I do believe the old buzzard's really upset.

'What could I do? I implored. But in the face of such betrayal.'

'Stop acting. She worships you and since Dora came you've treated her appallingly.'

'I've hardly seen the woman. What could I have done to her?'

'Quite. You've ignored her. And when she's gone you'll make the most terrible fuss.'

'Gone?' Such desolation in the echo of a word. Could that be the glint of a tear on his cheek? Hard to tell in winter's tea-time twilight. He is dying. Not today or tomorrow, but in this awful room, stuffy, the litter-tray stinking of cat, mess of papers, debris of a disordered imagination, dying he is. The tent of shadow folds in on him and yet I cannot take his hand.

At least let him get up, let him stay, play his games, have his whisky, his Dora, his cats, his fancies. We should be able to bear it. Just for this moment I can imagine that we might.

In the near-darkness Virginia found it easier to ask.

'Father, does it help, believing—what you do?'

'Knowing that I am a prisoner of lives everlasting? Sometimes it has. Curiosity, the hope each time of something better to come. But that's worn thin. I want to be free.'

'Free? What would that mean? Some nirvana?'

'I used to think. Now my best hope's extinction.'

'Not you.'

He snatched at something in her voice.

'You were always my favourite, Ginny. You know that?'

She shook her head, not denying but not to be caught in his mesh.

'I'm changing my will.'

'Oh yes.'

'Don't you want to know?'

'No.'

Oliver had lost her, he knew it. He plucked at the bedspread and followed her with his gaze as she turned on the bedside lamp, opened the top of the window a crack and pulled the curtains. What he didn't see was that there were tears in her eyes.

'I'm a trouble to you all,' he said (did his lower lip tremble?). 'It won't be long, I can tell. I can always tell.'

'Don't be absurd.' Virginia picked up a fallen pillow. 'Just try to be nice to Humble and tell me when you want to get up.'

Outside, Virginia leaned against the closed door.

'Damn you,' she breathed, closed her eyes and said again, 'Damn you.'

Oliver took flight and hovered. A couple of the most resolute stone-watchers had actually set up a tent half-way up the hill. There seemed to be a male, a female and an infant. By moonlight, it was hard to make out much more, though he could see that they had a fire going, contained in some way. It was a consoling sight, the fire—small brave evidence of life on the dark hillside.

10

'Where were you? I could tell you weren't asleep.'

'Eh?' Oliver blinked. Returning, he found Dora sitting by his bed.

'You were at the throne, weren't you?'

'As it happens, yes.'

'They'll catch you nipping out like that one day, you know. Or, rather, they'll find your body in bed and think you're in a coma.'

Oliver shrugged. By the single lamp, Dora looked magnificent. She had loosened her hair and it fanned out to her shoulders and framed her face in an aureole of electric gold; when she brushed it, it crackled. By this light, her pink nose was not in evidence. She wore Oliver's old Jaeger dressing-gown draped over her shoulders, as a cloak. A memory teased Oliver—an over-ripe fig in a blue bowl on a wooden table; a woman seated at the table, dreaming, a hair-brush in her hand. Heat.

'I remember—' he said; but it was gone.

'We could go together, one day,' Dora whispered. 'We could fly. Anywhere. We could go now. Do you remember loving me? Do you love me?'

'I have forgotten. I think I have forgotten how to love.'

'Did you know,' she murmured, 'that the foetus dreams?'

He closed his eyes and imagined how, even before sight, images might flash upon the soul's retina. How astonishing! This could be a dream, all this present life, those before, the island, the planet, even the universe itself—the fancies of his sleeping brain. Visions between the white silences of dreamless sleep.

Hic incipit vita. When would be the awakening? When would life begin?

'A sort of humming noise.'

Virginia rang Sam.

'And people are coming. There's even someone camped there. They want to interview father. It's building up.'

'What you wanted, surely? Good publicity to save the site?'

'Umm. I'm not sure it's all good.'

'What's this about a noise?'

'Oh, nothing. Hold on.' Virginia shut the study door and picked up the receiver again. 'Sam, do you believe in reincarnation?'

'What? No. Ginny, are you all right?'

'Yes, fine, really. I was just ringing in case you knew where Sandy was. He's gone off. He's not with you?'

'Hardly.'

'No, I suppose not.'

'I'm sure you needn't worry.'

'No. He just had a quarrel with Dora, that's all. He'll be in Balham.'

'Ginny?'

'Yes?'

'This fuss about the stone—I think you ought to keep Oliver out of it, if you don't want a circus.'

'Try to keep Father out of anything. How's Lucy?'

'Fine. Missing you.'

'Me too.'

'Love.'

'Yes.'

Virginia laid the receiver back in its rest. She was reluctant to break contact yet she could not have explained to Sam what, precisely, troubled her. A vague apprehension—no more, she supposed, than we all live with now. And she was tired, it was winter, she missed Sam and Lucy, worried about Sandy.

She tackled Oliver.

'Well, if you're going to do this interview, you'd better get up. But are you sure it's a good idea? Seeing this man, I mean?'

'I shall get up and I shall be interviewed. I shall get up for Sunday lunch.'

Virginia nodded. At least it would give them a chance to air the room.

That night, Oliver doubled his secret exercise routine.

In Balham at night Sandy dreamed of Dora. Once she was so close, he could have sworn she rested on the air above his bed, in the attitude of someone reclining on a sofa. In his dream he reached up and touched her hair. She smiled. His finger-tips tingled.

He woke confused and exhausted. By day he walked the streets, but even in sunshine, London and all her beauties were distanced, seen through clouded glass; and the hum he had noticed his first day away from the island, would not be silenced—it was in his head, it was his head, his mind, his reason. In exchange for chores and baby-sitting Gloria fed him, or he might have starved.

It was a period of no-weather, when on the island thin mist and cloud seemed to join, to be parted only briefly round mid-day by a pale silver sun. In the London parks the birds stood still on monochrome branches and railings; wood appeared dead, iron was cold. On a bench in Battersea Park Sandy picked up a newspaper. It was a small paragraph on page two:

Islanders plagued by Mystery Hum
Ministry of Defence denies secret weapon

Doctors were apparently divided on the subject of hysterical tinnitus. Animal welfare groups were unable to explain why dogs but not cats were affected. The only point on which all were agreed was that the sound emanated from the granite outcrop at the highest point of the island, known as Cerdic's throne. Both the stone and plot—readers were reminded—had lately been put up for sale by the Church Commissioners, and were at the centre of a controversy involving preservationists and other pressure groups.

Sandy tore out the cutting, folded it and put it in his pocket. He took out the biscuit he had saved from last night for lunch. He could have made himself a sandwich at Gloria's, he knew, or he had brought enough money to buy one (he felt guilty about that—he had spent no time at all alone with his grandmother yet Kitty, kissing him goodnight, had slipped £5 into his top pocket); but some fancy, or deeper need, had possessed Sandy to live as though he had nothing and needed nothing. He felt what he recognised to be a Dostoevskian urge to do penance. He remembered from the polytechnic nineteenth-century literature course he had abandoned to follow Dora to Rome that Charlotte Brontë had, on impulse, confessed herself at a Catholic church in Brussels. If he didn't guess he would make a fool of himself he would have done the same. Perhaps he should do the same for the self-abasement of making a fool of himself?

Close to his feet, a sparrow hopped, pecking, it seemed, at crumbs of dust. Of what great sin am I guilty? Sandy wondered and could think of none, and yet this weight was on him. Gloria, who had her own problems,

146

had noticed. 'Smile, man, the end of the world was yesterday,' she said, as she slapped and kissed her younger children off to school, and Sandy had smiled and felt shamed. She had taken it that he was moping for Dora—as, of course, he was—but there was more to it than that. He envied Dora, who never felt guilty about anything. How did she manage it? Was there something abnormal about him, that he couldn't take life lightly, as if he were responsible for the crimes of mankind? So instead of fighting for Dora, he ran off like a fugitive who deserves nothing better than exile. Because happiness always astonished him, when it came his way he gave it up too easily.

What were they up to now, Sandy wondered, Dora and his grandfather, at this minute? They could be here, listening to his thoughts, presences at his shoulder, unseen and laughing. He clenched his fists.

From right to left, across the charcoal picture, an old woman passed, pushing a dog in a pram. The woman wore a grey coat tied with string, and plastic summer sandals. All the time she pushed, she talked to the grey-muzzled mongrel, who sat up straight with an air of long-suffering acceptance. It was hard to tell from the woman's tone if she were scolding or loving.

Sandy turned his head. He had been conscious of a movement at the corner of his vision, and now saw a girl walking quickly from the children's playground. There was something about the way she walked, the set of her shoulders; she might have been wearing a cloak. Before

147

Sandy could get to his feet she was gone and the arcs of the empty swing grew shorter until soon it was still. Sandy thought of running but decided against it. A trickle of grey light turned the river to dangerous mercury, iron too, and the paler, more fragile silver of domes and tower-block windows. Sandy ate half the biscuit and crumbled the other half for the sparrow, which did not even so much as hop aside when he stood and walked briskly off, as though he knew where he were going.

That night he asked Gloria, 'Do you believe in magic?'

Hum. Confusion.

The sprouts were overcooked, Humble had dropped the best vegetable dish, and Mag's gang of hounds had poured unleashed from the van, terrorising Pippa's children, Oliver's cats and Ralph's dog. The cats retreated, swearing, out of their reach, Pippa's infants screamed and clung to her skirts. Only brave little Jackie stood his ground, barking, for a moment at least, before he too took flight, leading the pack through the house, round the garden and back again.

Virginia yelled for Mag to shut up the dogs.

'Come on, chaps, we're not wanted.'

'Mag, for heaven's sake. Just put them in the shed and get yourself a drink.' Virginia was momentarily ashamed —if Pippa brought her children why shouldn't Mag have her dogs? Pippa's children didn't bark, but they bit and chased cats. Lucy was terrified of them—they pulled limbs off her dolls, ate peanut butter at any time of day from the pot until they were sick and alarmed her with their precocious carnal knowledge. Pippa and Eric did not lock the bathroom door.

Eric was in the garden with Ralph, discussing the fruit trees in a kind of stationary drizzle that was more air than precipitation. What short legs he has, thought Virginia as she stood, hands in hot suds, but then so has Pippa; two peg-people that seem to fit exactly, into each other, into the earth. They should have nothing to do with the likes of us that frown in our sleep and dash around, pursued, pursuing, snatching bright rags from the air; blow on us and we crumble to dust. They endure.

Pippa took the children out into the garden. Mag, dogless, stomped back into the kitchen. Through the window they could see Pippa's son Saul stalking an unwary cat—a younger one who had failed to heed dog-eared Priam's example or Alcestis's sharper advice. He snatched it up by the armpits and bore it away, scratching at the air. Mag snorted.

'The more I see of the human race, the better I like our four-legged friends. You're out of whisky.' She sat down heavily at the kitchen table.

'Father must have finished it. I think Humble smuggles it up to him. No reason why he shouldn't have it, of course, but he does love plots.'

'What's this all in aid of anyway? His birthday's not till December.'

Virginia looked up from basting the joint.

'Didn't I say? It's a sort of *levée*—he's coming down-stairs—or that's the idea.'

'Why?'

Virginia laughed, closed the oven door and sat down at the table. Mag had brought in two tumblers of sherry—'All I could find.'

'That's what I wondered—about him getting up, I mean. Something to do with this interview, I suppose. The television people are coming this week.'

'Local?'

'No—a national thing. *This England.* One of those programmes they put on so late you never see the whole of it. Quite good, really, if predictable. Thin men with wispy beards standing in ploughed fields—you know. Oh, of course, you don't do you.' Mag had no television because, she said, Barbara Woodhouse was cruel to dogs. Stubbing out her cigarette, Virginia thought, I wish I could ask Mag if she is happy. I wonder how lonely she was when we were children.

'Sherry always makes me want to snivel. I'd better get on. Wherever is Humble now?'

Humble was standing in the cabbage patch with her friend. Mary didn't seem to feel wet feet, but of course, she wouldn't, being of the spirit. Humble had felt the same on her little trips with Sir Oliver, before the others came. It had been nice, the travelling—like dreaming but more real.

Mary said she'd no need to be so upset about the

150

vegetable dish. They put upon her, Mary considered. She should either go or stand up for her rights. She spoke gently, as you would expect, but she was quite firm.

Susan Humble felt much better. She could say anything to her friend, more than to anyone she had ever known. Almost, she thought of telling her about the travelling man, who had touched her cheek and brought her flowers, and how she still thought of him sometimes. But there was no need, because Mary understood everything, without telling.

Perhaps when they knew one another better, she might ask Mary about her Son? Not the cruel part, but if she was with Him now and could talk to Him? If He was company and comfort for her, or was that not allowed, bearing in mind who His father was?

When Mary put her hand on Humble's arm you could see that it wasn't smooth and white like the pictures but wrinkled like anyone else's, just as if she still did the washing-up.

Humble was happy. She had never had a best friend before, even at school.

Pippa's children were diverted now: pelting one another with fallen apples. Pippa came into the kitchen with the smallest lolling on her hip.

'What's Mrs Humble doing in the cabbage patch?'

Virginia pushed back her hair, transferred the joint from roasting-tin to plate, put the serving plate back in the oven and the tin on top, to make gravy.

'Cutting a cabbage?'

'No, just standing and muttering.'

'She must be sulking about the vegetable dish, though I told her it didn't matter. This house gets more like a Russian play every day. All we need is a cherry orchard and a gunshot offstage. Where's father? It's nearly ready. And Flora-Dora of the lily-white hands?'

'I'll call them.'

'Won't come down? What do you mean?' Virginia looked blankly at Dora.

'He says he won't come down because Sandy's not here.'

'But he hardly spoke to Sandy when he was here.'

'Well, that's what he says.'

Dora, her message delivered, awarded Virginia one of her smiles, second-class. While the weather was less cold, she had reverted from her blankets to the grey cardigan in which she had arrived, together with high boots and a number of rings that looked as though they had come from Christmas crackers. Pippa had at least been forewarned but Eric, who had never seen Dora before, stood at the sideboard momentarily frozen, carving knife and fork in his hands.

Virginia shrugged. She had expected this. 'Oh well. Better send a plate up then. Dora, this is my brother-in-law, Eric; Eric, Dora Phenicule.'

Eric blushed and carried on carving.

Mag peg-legged her way across the uncarpeted floor

as though on wooden stumps. Stripped of her dogs, she was diminished, just an awkward middle-aged woman, shy as a schoolgirl.

For years the dining-room had hardly been used and it did not welcome. The furniture was exactly as Virginia remembered it from childhood: large and dark and cruel. Most massive and threatening of all was the empty carver chair at the head of the table. All tried not to look at it, but it would not be shunned. In the end, as the plates were passed and Ralph poured his decent house-guest wine, it was Kitty who said,

'Olly's very much here when he isn't, don't you think?'

No one answered. Saul spilled his Ribena. Pippa said, 'Gosh, I'm sorry,' and while she went to fetch a cloth, Saul drank his mother's wine.

Virginia said, 'The sprouts are overcooked.'

Pippa came back, mopped the table and took her wineglass away from Saul. Saul screamed.

'Oh dear,' Pippa said, 'sorry. Honestly, Saul, I think you'd better eat in the kitchen with the others. They've got beefburgers with onion,' she added hopefully, im-ploring Eric with her gaze. Saul locked his legs round those of the chair. His face was puce—clearly he was holding his breath. Eric put down his knife and fork and napkin, got up from his place and with Pippa in atten-dance, carried Saul and chair bodily into the kitchen. The silence he left behind was tense.

'Not fit to bring up a dog,' uttered Mag, startling everyone.

Pippa came back. 'Sorry!'

Somehow or other, lunch was eaten. Doomed, it appeared, until Ralph opened a second and then a third bottle. Pippa stopped getting up to check that the children had not killed each other in the kitchen.

'This trifle's good,' she said. 'Not Mrs Humble, surely?' Virginia nodded. 'Someone must have helped her,' Pippa concluded.

The pitch of conversation rose. Virginia yawned and relaxed a little.

'Comice,' Ralph said.

Eric replied. 'Edwards.'

'But don't you think——'

Ralph really wanted to talk to Kitty. Was she avoiding him?

Kitty turned to Dora.

'Now tell me, my dear, about people leaving their bodies. It sounds so interesting. Are you able to do it, too?'

'Oh yes.'

'So you have travelled a lot?'

'Almost everywhere.'

'Such a saving!' And to be free, Kitty thought, of these bones. With the damp weather, her arthritis was at its worst.

'Travel,' Mag interjected abruptly. 'Never done it.'

'Winter spray,' said Eric.

Kitty continued. 'And can you tell me how it feels—when you are free, so to speak?'

Dora pondered, as she did any question.

'Granny Smith,' said Ralph to Eric.

'A Cox's man, myself.'

Is that thunder, Virginia wondered?

Oliver thumped the floor three times with his broom handle. Everyone looked up at the ceiling, except Dora, who pronounced into the silence.

'Orgasm,' she said, answering Kitty. OBE's like the best time you ever came.'

'Oh Lord,' said Virginia. 'Look!'

One of Mag's dogs passed the window with a cat in its mouth, Saul in pursuit and the whole pack at their heels.

Pippa left in tears. Mag maintained that since the cat was unhurt and it was known that dogs never caught cats, her hound was rescuing the animal from Saul's attentions. What was more, people who kept children should look after them. Pippa, in her opinion, was not fit to have a hamster.

This uncharacteristically long speech concluded, Mag called up her hounds and rattled off in her van. Pippa howled, Eric consoled her, Saul screamed, Jackie barked. He at least, locked in the toolshed, was innocent of all but hysteria.

The others stood in the damp drive to watch them go. The rain had stopped, to be replaced by grey mist that all but veiled the throne.

'Oh dear,' said Kitty, 'I had a feeling that something might happen.'

Dora went indoors, Ralph to the shed to quieten Jackie. Kitty and Virginia paused.

'Look at the throne. You can just see—there's someone camped there. In this weather. It's extraordinary how they keep coming.'

'People need magic, don't you think?' Kitty said; then she turned to go in. 'I must write a postcard to Minette.'

'Tell me then, my darling, are they all very cross?'

Alcestis—complacent as messenger and loved one—purred hummingly in Oliver's ear. Fleeing the drama downstairs, the whole gang had assembled in the bedroom and even as she lay warmly on Oliver's pillow, Alcestis held them at bay with sharp amber eye and claw sheathed but ready. When she was queen, only tattered Priam was allowed on the eiderdown—and then at a distance.

Oliver sighed. No one had come to fetch his lunch tray and the sprouts had been overcooked. Small thorns. The truth was, mischief was losing its bite. Having summoned them all here, he found that he was bored with games. He needed a grander diversion to distract him.

He remembered now that he had felt this lowness before. The spirit was open to it unless the end were sudden. Death was like birth—a leaving. He had been a man. He had feared his father, loved his wife, longed for a son, found this present earth sometimes beautiful.

Wake up! You're right, Alcestis my dear, to flick your tail. Expectation, attention and memory, says Augustine.

We've had enough of the first and the last. Now is the time for attention. Physical jerks for the brain: jump to it. Never mind, forget, past, future, passion, loss, a warm sun, ancient terrors, old tricks; let the sea take the prints of the boy's foot on the sand.

Regard the stone. Who is there? Cerdic? Or is it God that hums? Sod? Gog and Magog?

Is there no mind? Only the hum?

Concentrate!

Virginia answered the telephone.

'Ma?'

'Sandy! Wherever are you? Are you in Balham?'

'I've only got one tenpence. Is everything all right?'

'Yes, of course. Why shouldn't it be?'

'Nothing. I just wondered.'

'Grandfather's going on telly. If he'll get up. They're recording the day after tomorrow—*This England*. Sandy, reverse the charges. Is something wrong? Do you want to speak to Dora?'

'She's not in London is she?'

'No. How could she be? She's here.'

'And nothing's happened?'

'I told you. Well, nothing more than usual. For heaven's sake, Sandy, are you ill? What are you doing?'

'I'm thinking.'

The tenpence ran out and Virginia was left holding the receiver. Outside the telephone box Sandy stood in the grey rain. 'Dora?' he said and turned as he heard laughter, but saw only strangers in the busy street. To his right there was a church, to his left a newsagent. 'God?' he said, looking up at the blackened building. He ran through the graveyard that had become a rubbish tip but the door was locked; the windows that had once held stained glass were boarded up and London's pink weed which years ago had lent the city's bomb-sites a kind of grace now invaded even the porch. There were signs here of a fleeting occupancy—empty bottles, newspapers, a piece of sacking.

At the newsagent's Sandy bought the *Radio Times* and got change. Back in the telephone box he made one call. For the rest of the day until evening he walked blindly the Godless, Doraless streets.

'Sorry?' Ralph lifted his head. He had missed Oliver's remark. The truth was, he felt uncomfortable in Oliver's room. How do you say to your oldest friend in the world—and December to December, friends were thinning out every year—I have designs upon your wife, whom you have treated abominably; I doubt if she'll have me but if she will I'll take her. When we were young I kissed her on the beach and I have loved her ever since. 'I'm sorry. What did you say?'

'Yeats. Apposite.'

'Yes? In what way?'

' "*I would that the boar without bristles had come from the West/And had rooted the sun and moon and stars out of the sky/And lay in the darkness, grunting, and turning to his rest.*" '

158

'You've got me there. What's it all about?'

Ralph thought his friend looked a little flushed. Not necessarily ill, although it was hard to tell as he had barely seen him since he arrived. It was probably the heat of the room. Shocking smell of cat to Ralph's dog-man's nose.

'Longing for the world to end,' Oliver said. 'Think of that—to perish and take it with you!'

Ralph touched his moustache.

'That seems a pity. Not such a bad place, I'd say, all in all. I rather enjoy it. You used to, too.'

Oliver grunted.

'Ralph, what do we do about the throne?'

Ralph stretched his leg. So that's it, he thought without malice—he wants something. He always did.

'I can look into it, but there's not much, I'm afraid. The National Trust would have been our best bet, but they can't afford it. As for protest, public opinion's a queer old horse to ride—politicians don't like it, you know, it bothers them. Civil servants regard it as a personal affront. But it's all we've got. You do your best on the box, we may carry the day.' Privately, Ralph had little hope of this. Once, Oliver might have had the power to sway. We are grown old.

Ralph stood, rubbing his leg. Just time to walk Jackie before dinner. It was dark already, and outside, the blackness of the night seemed to thicken, to take on the texture of fur. Jackie was unusually reluctant to take his airing, ran round the lawn and returned to Ralph's side.

No sun, no moon, no stars. Just the hum. Although it was not cold, Ralph shivered. He touched Jackie and found that the dog was trembling. They went indoors.

Humm.

Sandy had slipped past Gloria's door unnoticed and lay now in the dark on the narrow bed. He was glad to be hungry and uncomfortable, for at last he grasped that the indefinable guilt he had felt in Battersea Park had been anticipatory—shame for a crime he had only today committed. It hardly mattered if the BBC took his revelations seriously or not. Maybe they would dismiss Oliver as a crank and cancel the interview. The point was, in his conscience Sandy had betrayed his grandfather because he believed Oliver had taken Dora from him and he was jealous.

He shifted his position. His hip-bones were so sharp it was quite painful to lie on them. It was interesting about guilt, Sandy thought. His act might have no repercussions at all and yet he felt the greatest sinner. Sternly he examined himself for masochism, but there was no pleasure in this self-abnegation. What was more, he knew quite well that, even if no one found him, he would never have the courage to lie here till he died. He could try though, for a while—a night and a day perhaps?

That night no angel or daemon came, no Dora, to shrive or to curse him, or to make his fingers tingle and tease him with her hair. Not even from below, Gloria's glorious orgasms to remind and punish him.

At two o'clock in the morning Sandy crept downstairs and stole half a loaf of sliced bread from Gloria's kitchen. On second thoughts, he added a banana, a pot of peanut butter and a knife.

11

Alcestis had got out of bed the wrong side this morning and perpetrated a clumsy theft. Normally a selective and cunning burglar, adept at covering her tracks, this time she had snatched a pheasant from the larder and having messed it about, left the kitchen a battlefield of blood and feathers.

Flung out of the house, she had taken station on the woodshed roof. From here—amber eyes baleful—she glared through the window at Virginia's attempts to clean up.

'Well, we can't eat it now,' Virginia said to Kitty, 'and if I put it in the dustbin she'll just get it out again. I'd better wait till tonight and bury it in the garden. I can't think what got into her. And what a day to choose!'

Kitty sipped her Gold Blend Nescafé made with milk. It was the nearest she could get to that lovely French pale tepid breakfast coffee.

'I expect she realised there was something going on. She probably doesn't like Oliver getting up. Cats know, I always think—dogs merely dote.' Not for the first time lately, Kitty was pleasurably surprised by her calm in the face of situations that only a few weeks ago, in some other life, would have brought on an attack of gnats in the head. She had weathered even that frightful scene on Sunday with equanimity. Had she undergone a sea-change, she wondered? Or was this an unlooked-for blessing of age (the only one she could think of)—a sense of detachment from life's little fusses? Possibly Olly felt like this when he left the body.

She plucked a pheasant feather from her saucer. How pretty.

'Oh look, there's the postman. Good gracious, Alcestis seems to have gone for him. She's hanging onto his trouser leg. How extraordinary! She must be very cross about something.'

While Virginia went to release the postman Kitty finished her coffee and thought of Minette. It was rather silly writing to her, she realised that. If only someone would invent catnip postcards! Perhaps they had?

There was only one piece of mail and Humble, just arrived and still dressed in her outdoor clothes, gave it to Kitty with the menacing air of someone handing over a letter-bomb. Poor woman, Kitty thought, she does look so like a black parcel. And all these years she has had this crush on Olly. Yet there is something about her—especially lately—that defies pity. There are people like that: so utterly themselves, one's attitude to them seems irrelevant.

Kitty looked at the letter. Since she could think of no

one who might be writing to her, her first thought was of Minette. Not that even such a cultivated cat could write, but she might be ill, the letter could be from Britt.

The stamp however was English and now she put on her spectacles, Kitty could see that the postmark was London. Some intuition persuaded her to take it to the privacy of the sewing-room.

Sandy had written with biro, rather shakily, on cheap lined paper that looked as though it had been taken from a school exercise book.

Dear Grannie I am writing to you because I have done something I know is wrong and could cause trouble. It doesn't matter what it is as you can't do anything about it, but I have to tell someone. My friends here have their own problems and parents always think they are to blame. So please don't say anything to my mother. Don't worry—I'm all right—but I'm not sure if I'll come back. I've been thinking a lot lately, more than I ever have in my life, and I haven't finished. I don't suppose I ever will! One of the things is about who I really love and who I ought to love. It's very complicated. I love you, I know, and Dora, but I'm not old enough, or not young enough any more, to be sure about my parents. And there's a lot I feel guilty about. For ages I didn't know why. Perhaps I had to do one bad thing to have a reason for feeling like this?

It's the middle of the night so I could catch the first post, but I probably won't send it. If I do, please forgive all this rubbish and don't show it to anyone. It's just helped a bit to talk to you. Do you remember, we used to have the same dreams?

Sorry this is all about me.

Love,
Sandy

Thoughtfully, Kitty put the letter back into the envelope and the envelope into the knitting bag which—since her arthritis—rarely carried knitting but had become a holdall from which she was rarely separated. She could not remember when she had last been so touched. Ralph's declaration of love had been startling, exciting, wild, but Sandy's confession moved her almost to tears. How long since she had wept. What unlooked-for turns her life had taken since she came to the island. She dabbed her eyes. Whatever next?

Alcestis the criminal had infiltrated over the greenhouse roof through Oliver's bedroom window and crouched now, disapproving, on top of the tallboy, her fur spiked and furious with rain.

'No use, my dear,' said Oliver, 'I shall do as I like.'

The secret exercises had paid off and he felt strong, quite spritely. Ralph had offered help which he refused and Humble—about as prickly today as Alcestis—had brushed and laid out his remaining suit. Oliver surveyed it. Funeral gear, he decided, and rejected it in favour of a smoking-jacket he had bought in Istanbul in 1935.

Lichen-coloured to begin with, it now bore the verdigris bloom of time, neglect and English wardrobes by the sea. To this he added a spotted red silk scarf, knotted inside his shirt as a cravat.

Dora knocked.

'Are you ready? There are men downstairs with dirty feet and cables they're laying all over the place. They look like burglars. I say, that gear's incredible. You couldn't buy it for anything now if you tried. Very sexy.'

Oliver was pleased. 'You are a tiresome child.'

'I know.'

Humble had never thought where television came from. In fact, she preferred not to speculate, assuming simply that these were spirits of the ether marginally less solid than her friend, the Virgin. Well, of course, you saw pictures of them mowing the lawn and entertaining informally but that was another plane of their existence, and one with which she was not concerned. Even the letter from Richard Baker thanking her for the Fair Isle sweater was less real than his face on the screen. Then she knew he was talking to her personally, even though other people were listening in. Now she had got to know her better she put this to the Virgin Mary, who confirmed that the air was full of spirits. If you had eyes to see or ears to hear them, there were far more than there were people. So when she, Humble, and Sir Oliver, left their bodies, they were behaving in a perfectly normal way.

Last night, Susan Humble, thinking of Miss Trouble,

Dora, had asked her friend if there were bad spirits who interfered with decent people's lives.

Mary smoothed her blue robe. She was so calm and gentle, the canary would perch quietly on her hand. This evening they had been watching the Monday-night film on BBC 1 and the Virgin had not been at all shocked by the violence. Because she was so serene and sensible, you sometimes forgot that she had been there on Good Friday as well as at Christmas and the Annunciation. She had seen them hammer the nails into His hands and there had been no Lord's Prayer, no Church, nothing to comfort her then.

'Well, I'm not very clever,' Mary said, 'but I believe there are some spirits better avoided. They might be not so much wicked as naughty. I lead a quiet life though, so I couldn't be sure. If you are thinking of someone in particular, I'd say that as a spirit, she is not very mature. She is still of the earth too, and it takes time to learn not to play. Not that you have ever abused *your* gift, my dear.'

Humble was touched. If it had been in her nature, she would have felt proud. She made a cup of tea, though her friend—like those nuns who bake a cake for you and can't eat in company—could never share the pot, and asked about the Archangel Gabriel, if he had made Mary jump.

And now, here were all these people stamping through the house without wiping their feet, upsetting the electricity and wanting black coffee and not using ash-trays and sending the cats crazy and some who didn't have anything to do at all but the Union said they had to be there and it wasn't even Richard Baker but some female person. It wasn't television as Humble thought of it. She plonked down the tray and retired to the kitchen. Opening the larder door, she nearly screamed. There was something dead in it, which on closer inspection turned out to be a pheasant. It looked as if it had been murdered.

'Sanctuary,' said Oliver, presenting his best profile. He was beginning to enjoy himself. He wondered why he had never done this before. In some forgotten life he must surely have been an actor, it came so naturally to him to perform. The polite attention as the question was put to him, the moment of reflection, the thoughtful answer. 'A refuge,' he explained. 'For centuries Cerdic's throne has been regarded by the ignorant as a place of safety.' He made a steeple of his hands. 'Although it frequently distorts, folklore may sometimes point the way to historical fact.'

Barbara, Brenda—whatever her name was—crossed her legs. A fine pair, Oliver judged, strong too. No beauty, but promising legs worn well were often an indication of sensuality more significant than a pretty face. When he was a dwarf in Silesia he had chosen his mistresses entirely from the aspect below the waist, rejecting many a more conventional feature.

168

Alcestis shifted in his lap. While the rest of the household was banished, she had slipped in on his heels and Miss Legs had said she could stay. She would have stayed anyway.

'I'm sorry? You were saying?'

'Why is it so vital that the throne should be preserved?'

'Ah yes.' Oliver threw back his head, then lowered it. He gave her the Anglo-Saxon heritage, the blood that flows in our veins of a civilisation so much richer than most appreciate. The great burial mounds he summoned—the bronze, the horn set with jewels, the treasures of the dead chieftain; he invoked the burning of Cerdic's castle, the poetry of the wanderer banished from the empty hall. How that time had gone for the exile from the hearth, vanished under the helm of night as though it had never been, says the poet. *Niht-helm* that swallows all.

He was carried away. He could feel Alcestis's purr in his lap. To Hell with scholarship. Stand with the doomed *Bretwalda*, the king of Britain, founder of the house of Wessex, at the stone; granite glinting with mica.

'How can we let that go?'

'Can you explain the hum that has troubled the island's residents?' Swish of legs recrossed. 'That seems to come from the stone?'

'Cerdic's voice.'

'So you are one of those, Sir Oliver, who believe it to be—for lack of a better word—a *magic* place?' Swift smile.

At the word 'magic', Alcestis stiffened. So did Oliver, regretting that last swig from the Milpar bottle.

'I consider that we live as untutored barbarians in a universe of infinite possibilities.'

Miss Legs demurely glanced at the clipboard on her lap. 'Would reincarnation be one of those possibilities?'

Alcestis stiffened as she did when confronted by an impertinently casual bird.

Oliver answered, 'Presumably.'

'Is it true that you yourself have undergone re-incarnation?'

'I really do not see—'

'You have had paranormal experiences?'

'Given that normal is a subjective and suburban definition, paranormal has no meaning.'

'But you admit that you have left your body and flown without mechanical support?'

Oliver frowned before he answered. 'Yes.' It was at that moment that Alcestis gathered her haunches and leaped from Oliver's lap. It appeared almost that she flew. Claws unsheathed and anchored on fifteen-denier micromesh, she bit Miss Legs hard, twice, on the calf.

'Christ!' said Virginia, watching that evening in company with Kitty, Ralph and Dora. They had cut the flying cat but otherwise the interview was horrifyingly intact. 'Where did they get it from? It certainly wasn't any of us. You don't think Humble? She's been very odd lately.'

'Oh, I don't think so,' said Kitty emphatically.

170

Uneasily, she was remembering Sandy's letter of confession.

'No, I suppose not.' Virginia turned off the set. 'She dotes on Father. I must say he took it quite well—better than that Barbara creature at being bitten. I never thought I'd have a good word for Alcestis but I wouldn't have minded biting her myself.'

The telephone rang. Mag—who had seen it in the pub—wanted to know if Father had finally gone off his chump. Pippa was breathless and anxious, as if having a flying father were in the same category as an outbreak of Hong Kong flu. Given half a chance, she would have brought over home-made soup. The next call was from the *Daily Express*, followed by a woman who announced herself as the Witch of Walthamstow. Virginia left the telephone off the hook.

In the hall she found Ralph standing at the front door, while Jackie had his last outing.

'Fog,' he said. 'Never seen it so thick.'

Now they were alone, Kitty turned to Dora. If she reflected, she knew she would never speak, and this had to be said. One should not be shy of people simply because they were peculiar. Besides, who was to say what was peculiar nowadays? The world might be full of Doras, for all Kitty knew; by next summer coachloads of Doras debouching in the *place* at St Marie. And in a surprising way she had grown quite fond of the girl, remembering her seagull mews in the Mediterranean night. She took a deep breath.

'My dear, I have to ask you an impertinent question.

Only because I care for my grandson very much. Do you love him?'

Dora put down her knitting. 'Yes.'

'Good. Then I think you should either go to him or fetch him back here. He is unhappy. I believe you know where he is?'

The girl nodded.

'That's settled then. I'm so glad.'

Kitty smiled. With this off her mind, she realised how tired she was. It was late. On the way to her room she passed the stairs that led to Oliver's bedroom. She could have sworn she heard him laugh.

Tonight of all nights, Susan Humble was glad of Mary's company; even if, for some reason, the Virgin would not quite sit down but seemed to have settled somewhere in mid-air between the chair and the ceiling.

Humble had told her about the business of the pheasant and the television people and Alcestis, and then they watched the programme together at 10.35. Either the hum or the fog, or perhaps the presence of spirits, interfered with the picture, so that Sir Oliver seemed to have his own shadow or it might have been his soul, sitting behind him.

The shock was terrible. Oliver had told no one the content of the interview, simply unhooked Alcestis from Miss Legs and stalked up to his tower.

Humble gasped then was astonished to hear the Virgin laugh. In fact, she actually clapped her hands.

172

'But dear friend, don't you see? How splendid to have someone speak out for the soul! Such a comfort to those who doubt and to other spirits.'

Still anxious, Humble thought that, after all, Mary was sometimes as innocent as she was painted. In her own opinion, secrets were better kept. The world had a way with them that was not always nice. And then there was the possibility of blasphemy. Or was it sacrilege?

'You don't think that He will mind? It's not that Sir Oliver could be called, you might say, religious. That is'—she lowered her voice—'I have heard him mock Father and Son.'

'Heavens,' said Mary cheerfully, 'don't you think we have enough of the other sort? All those cold churches! Everyone so miserable about it, poor little bodies all cramped up with sin. And worse—the things that are done in His name. He had hoped so much for kindness and joy.' Mary clasped her hands. 'Do you know one of the most blessed things I ever saw? Nuns dancing! They were very young—novices—and they were cleaning a chapel on a spring morning, the doors open, the sun streaming in, when one began to hum and then another, and then there they were, holding hands and dancing, in and out of the aisles and on the altar. They were so pretty. It was a little French song they had learned in the world. I could hum it to you now.'

Like the Cheshire cat, the Virgin began to fade, as she often did when she saw that Humble was tired—a

173

friend tactfully taking her leave, though her smile remained.

In Balham everyone was out but Sandy, the chief of sinners, who crouched before Gloria and Gregory's television. Officially he was baby-sitting. In fact, perched on the maroon divan with an untouched portion of Kentucky fried chicken, he was in the dark night of the soul. The weather was suitable. London no longer has fogs but in the still, dark, damp times that would once have produced a pea-souper in which whores might be strangled and bodies slipped into the lower reaches of the Thames, there gathers a miasma becoming to tormented spirits and their scourges. If there were a God and He were vengeful, and He had a hound, He would sniff me out tonight, Sandy thought. He shuddered, imagining the Holy Dog at the door.

'Life's a dog, honey.' That was what Gloria had said when she finally cornered him. Why wasn't he eating? What was he doing up there alone all night? Was it a row with Dora? Sandy nodded, for that was, after all, in part, the truth. Let it go. Comfort me not with Gloria.

Even when the programme was finished, Sandy, transfixed with horror, did not move to switch off the set. The hum that filled his skull was now so strong it blotted out the late news headlines. Grandfather had carried it off well, that was something, he supposed. In fact, with the air of an elegant and desiccated lizard, you could say he had triumphed.

174

Did that make Sandy's deed any less awful? He didn't know. Can the gravity of a sin be measured by its consequences? He suspected not. In any case, the damage was yet to be seen. And he had lost Dora for ever, that was certain.

It was at that moment that Dora appeared on the television screen. Jan Leeming simply faded though she went on talking, and there in her place, with her endless neck and Jeanne Hébuterne conical hair-style, was Dora. Smiling. Just for Sandy. It was wonderful, as though they were alone together, as though all were forgiven or perhaps there had never been very much to forgive. It was magic.

12

*T*here were consequences.

Frank Farmer, the front-man for *This England* who had been seen at the beginning of the programme lounging in the lap of the throne, circling the throne in a thin drizzle behind streamers of sea mist, pacing from the throne to the edge of the cliff and back to the throne, a lock of pale hair plastered to his monkish features, holding forth about the throne, caught a cold. He became aware of a persistent hum in his head, which he put down to catarrh, except that when the cold was gone the hum remained. He was also one of the first pilgrims.

Ex-diplomat flies high screamed the *Express*, while on the home news page *The Times* recorded with seemly restraint in two column inches that the amateur historian and preservationist, Sir Oliver Hartley, appearing on BBC 1's *This England*, had admitted to having undergone paranormal experiences. On *Nationwide* two experts—a cleric and an academic psychologist—were given three

176

minutes to squabble about the parapsychology of out-of-body experience and the physico-chemical properties of the soul. In Roehampton a chiropodist and father of five stepped from the top floor of a tower-block.

The Church Commissioners refused to speak to reporters but announced the sale of the throne and the land around it to the Ministry of Defence.

After a week the story was dead, except on the island, where they still came in increasing numbers—the lost and the lame, the innocent and the damned. The fearful, of whom there were so many nowadays, with their children and their tents and caravans. The ferries had never had such business in December and the guesthouses reopened.

'What do they want?' Virginia wondered.

'Hope, I expect,' said Kitty, 'like everyone.'

'So father's some sort of guru?'

'Something like that.'

'It's weird.'

'There'll be more on the twenty-second.' Neither Kitty nor Virginia had realised that Dora was in the room. She had this irritating gift of appearing at your elbow when you felt sure she was somewhere else. It was possible, the way things had been going lately, that she simply materialised.

'For Olly's birthday? How would they know that?' Kitty was puzzled.

'No,' Dora explained, 'the winter solstice. Like the summer. That's when the sun's furthest from the equator and seems to stand still.'

'Of course!' Virginia realised. 'The only times the sun shines through the hole in the stone at noon. That could be what it was for—astronomical calculations. Are they waiting for something to happen?'

'I expect so,' said Dora. She was sitting in the rocking-chair by the kitchen fire with Alcestis in her lap. Ever since the affair of the biting and the pheasant-snatch, the cat had been impossible with anyone but Dora or Oliver. Virginia was permitted to prepare her food but Dora had to offer it. She had become vocal and aggressive—screeching at nightmare phantasms no one else could see and terrorising the noble dog, Jackie, who had scars on his nose to prove it. Now, when she chose to stalk the house, tail high and tip twitching, eyes crossed with rage, the other cats scattered as if she were the devil.

'I think that animal's gone mad,' said Virginia. And when Dora had left the room: 'I wish Sandy would come and take her away.'

Kitty looked up from the crossword book which seemed the only literature available in the village store. What had four legs and complained, two words, eight letters and five?

'Alcestis?'

'Dora.'

'She's quite sensible really, in her own way. It depends where you start from.' Whatever animal could have five letters and four legs? Assuming the eight to be adjectival?

At the stove, Virginia put the lid on the noxious pan of cat dinner.

'Where do you start from?'

178

'The probability of the miraculous. Then it's amazing how things make sense. I've only just realised that.' Horse? Stoat?

'You mean she's some kind of saint? Or witch?'

'I wouldn't go as far as that,' Kitty said. 'More a catalyst, perhaps?' Tiger? What did tigers have to complain about? 'Or acolyte. Attendant, you know.'

'I'm beginning to think I don't know anything.' On her way out, Virginia paused at the window. Someone had actually parked their caravan in the lane outside the rectory. They'll be on the lawn next. Through the streaming rain she dimly glimpsed the stone and the encampments on the hill, the leeward side. Perhaps her mother was right. One should start again from ignorance and hope for revelation. She saw her soul as a cluttered attic emptied and swept clean. If only she could.

Alone, Kitty got it and triumphantly filled in the squares:

GROANING BOARD

A spark had come into Oliver's eye. He would be leaving soon, he felt, but meanwhile the drama had rejuvenated him. Or was it the tug of a new life he could sense, already, even before he had sloughed off the old? The moment of death is the moment of conception, yet still, as Dora had said, the foetus dreams.

He no longer sought oblivion.

Nor mischief.

Nor love.

Approaching something like pity, he viewed with dispassion himself: the frightened child in rectory rhododendrons, the would-be great lover, the old-fashioned sinner, the impresario of chaos. And beyond himself, the world, weary planet running down. Idiots, he could have told them, to squander such beauty. I have ridden the great gales of the universe above your silos and battlefields and playground killings and have seen an oasis.

Damn fools! Thank God, the plague-flea, for laughter.

'What's the joke?' Dora said.

'There are no jokes left.'

'You were laughing.'

'I can fart too.'

Standing at the window, she shrugged.

'You can see their lights. It must be cold out there. We could go? Just one flight together.'

She could no longer tease him, this mistress from another time. There would be others. Oliver felt a pang of indigestion which might have been regret. Kitty had not been able to live with the clamouring of those dead women. Would he meet her too again, pebbles on the beach of eternity, and would he love her better?

So Dora touched his fingers and they leaped from their bodies, circled the stone and coasted back gently down the hill. A man standing outside his caravan felt a breeze on his bare head and then it was gone. Dora smiled like a surfer on the hump of a wave before it breaks.

Alcestis was waiting, furious, on the conservatory

roof. Nothing would console her. She had been abandoned, betrayed, and suspected worse to come. Even when they had re-entered their bodies she refused Oliver's offering of mackerel pâté from his tuck-box under the bed. At the same time when servile Priam approached the dish, stomach flattened to the floor in obeisance, he got a box on the already tattered ears, claws out.

'Perhaps the hum's got to her, after all,' said Virginia. 'It does seem louder. I can only think with the radio on.'

Sitting at the kitchen table, Frank Farmer licked his finger. He had made the mistake of trying to stroke Alcestis. He smiled bravely and hoped the animal wasn't rabid. He had long legs, which he appeared to be able to cross twice, a stick-like body tapering to a narrow head and the expression of a gentle man in shock. Perhaps it was his appearance of harmlessness that had got him past the police car at the gate.

'Would you like some iodine?'

'Oh no. I'm sorry to impose.'

'Never mind. Perhaps you can tell us what it's all about? I mean why have you come? For that matter what are they all doing here? Before the police moved in we had twenty people a day at the door. Some mad as hatters, of course, but quite a few apparently sane. What do they want? My mother said hope. But how can Father give them hope? He won't talk to anyone. I do understand a little, I think, but it frightens me. To tell you the truth, I'm very tired and rather scared.' Why was she talking like this to a stranger, she wondered, topping up their glasses.

'We come humbly,' he said—with the same smile of sanctity he would, on the screen, bestow upon a promising cumulus. 'Some in penance. To save the throne. To save our souls. In the hope of some evidence that we have souls to save. Many in simplicity, not knowing why.'

'Yes.'

He touched her hand across the table and Virginia had a crazy impulse to seize his and cling to it. His smile was not, after all, sanctimonious, but kind. Better than kind—happy.

'My father's not a good man, you know. If they're expecting Elijah in the chariot—'

'Don't you see? It doesn't matter. It is not what happens or who does it, but what people make of it.' Virginia nodded. He looks like a heron, she thought. 'Take Christ,' Farmer went on. 'Does it matter who He really was? Even if He existed?'

'I suppose not. But one's own father—'

Kitty came in.

'Have we any of that beef left over? Could I make sandwiches? And a thermos perhaps. There's a poor girl in the summerhouse with three children—one's a baby.'

'In the summerhouse?'

'Yes, they must be so cold too. I thought the oil-heater we had in the hall? Or even some blankets? Oh, I'm sorry.' Kitty noticed Farmer.

'Mother, this is Frank Farmer. You know, he did Father's programme.'

'Oh yes.' Kitty smiled. 'That must be *such* an interesting job.'

'Thank you. Well, actually, I've left the Beeb.'

'What a pity. I'm so sorry.' When he had gone, Kitty looked up from spreading Flora on a sliced loaf. 'Isn't it strange—when you see someone from television in real life, they don't seem quite real?' She went on happily spreading. Ralph had arrived now and was carving the beef. 'Like the royal family,' Kitty added. 'I once saw Queen Mary in Harrods and she looked like a pantomime dame.' Kitty was pleasantly surprised by her new-found energy. It was fun to be looking after people, for a change. Rather like the war. 'I think just four more slices, Ralph, and we'll be there. I wonder if she's feeding the baby herself. I must ask.'

'Mother,' Virginia said gently, 'we can't have people living in the summerhouse.'

'There, that's it! No. I'll take it, Ralph. I must find out about the baby. Do you think the policeman should have tea or beer?'

'I wish she'd let me do it,' Ralph said, watching Kitty anxiously as she crossed the lawn.

Virginia said, 'You're fond of Mother, aren't you?'

Shy, he touched his moustache. 'I love her very much.'

'And she?'

'I'm a dull old stick. Even if it weren't for Oliver.'

'You shouldn't let Father stand in your way.'

She had embarrassed him, she could see.

'I must get an aspirin. The hum's worse, don't you think?' On an impulse, Virginia kissed him quickly on the cheek. 'She ought to want you.'

He shook his head. 'I should be off.'

'Just stay till all this is over. You do help us, you know. Father breaks.' She searched for the word. 'You reconcile.'

Alone in the kitchen, Ralph took his station at the table, from which he could see the square of light on the lawn, waiting for Kitty.

The Church Commissioners were adamant. The Ministry of Defence, sore already from brushes with women and children tying up an air base with knitting wool, were puzzled by this new phenomenon as the Roman legion might have been at the mass hysteria engendered by the perfectly regular execution of one more Jewish anarchist. The island's welfare and sanitation services flapped their hands at the health hazards posed by this field of folk that stretched now from the rectory, up Poet's Walk to the throne. Sniffer police-dogs, confused by the hum, lost their noses for illegal substances, squatted on their haunches and howled. Dogs on the mainland joined in.

In the still, cold night, on the eve of the solstice—as Sandy hitched from Balham and Alcestis growled at the moon—only Oliver, still awake, and the insomniac dogs, were witness to a small miracle. Up Poet's Walk to the throne, stars that seemed to flower in a winding stream were the pilgrims' torches, while their bearers—heard even through the frosted glass—all at once joined in with the song of the throne, so the hum, humn, umnn, was the voice of the island and the earth and the sea and the sky; the deep-throated universe spoke.

Reaching even the sleepers.

Mag panted in nightmare, Pippa smiled in the arms of Eric, her orchard Adam. Ralph was a child again, lying in a field with his ear to the earth, while for Kitty roses fell out of a black sky. Virginia heard an old song in her sleep and was unaccountably happy. Sandy, dozing in the cab of a lorry on the way to the ferry terminal, dreamed of one single singing rose, a tight bud which opened and in its corolla was Dora's face.

Dora woke. She had been lying across the foot of Oliver's bed wrapped in cardigan, quilt and dressing-gown. Like a cat, she was immediately awake.

'What happens next?'

'It starts all over again.'

'Are you going?'

'Soon.'

'Can I come with you?'

'No.'

'What shall I do then? Love Sandy?'

'I imagine so.'

Turning to look at her, Oliver saw yet another wonder: she was standing beside him now at the window, the hair he still had a faint memory of loving fanned out below her shoulders, and down her cheek, as she watched the procession, there ran a single tear held in its own sac.

185

Would it break if he touched it? How would it taste? Even the Saint found his feet caught in the toils of this world's beauty.

Just as he bent to kiss her a raging fury came between them—not God but Alcestis fell apparently from the ceiling, spitting, with mad eyes crossed. Oliver opened the window, took her by the scruff, and dropped her on the conservatory roof. All night the jealous queen patrolled the window-sill, shaking with envy and cold.

Oliver slept in the armchair, sitting up, with Dora at his feet.

Humble had not turned up for two days. She had put a note through the door—presumably at dead of night since no one had seen her—to say that she had company and wouldn't be in. As dawn broke, she was trying to decide if her black shoes would do for the solstice, or should she wear the lamb-lined boots from last years sale? There might be some standing about and there was a hoar-frost. Every tree, every bush, every blade of grass was stiff with white. No use asking Mary. Humble hadn't even liked to look to see if her friend had feet.

Virginia studied the rounded biro letters on blue-lined paper.

'It's rather awful, I suppose, but I'd never thought of Humble as having friends. D'you think she's left for good?'

Kitty was still half in her dream of last night.

'As long as she doesn't come in like that maid in Anthony Powell, with nothing on. I had such a lovely dream.'

'How funny. So did I. Oh, Dora, there you are. Would you mind taking father's coffee up? And he seems to have a lot of birthday cards.' Dora looked tired, Virginia thought. Her skin seemed transparent and there were shadows under her eyes as if she hadn't been to bed. When she had left the kitchen, Virginia said, 'I'd never have believed it but I'm getting quite fond of Flora-Dora. Or perhaps I'm just used to her. Father seems to like her anyway.'

Kitty smiled vaguely. She was thinking of Ralph's declaration on that other frosty morning, and how the idea of loving him and being loved by him had seemed out of the question; yet the possibility must have been working within her for she had woken this morning—as though something had been settled in the night—to the conviction that she would accept him. She felt calm about this decision and so happy it would have been nice to tell Ginny—but that wouldn't be fair to Ralph.

'Oh dear! Poor Alcestis—but she does look splendid in a way.' Kitty opened the kitchen window to the remarkable vision of a hoar-frosted Alcestis. 'Are those icicles on her whiskers?'

Everything about the cat seemed frozen, even her temper. Virginia lifted her indoors where she stood, stiff and implacable.

187

'What do we do? Wait for her to thaw out? Can cats get frostbite?'

Virginia had gone for a towel from the warm rail by the range when Kitty exclaimed.

'Do look. There seems to be a lot of people in the lane. And there's that nice Mr Farmer. I wonder what they want.'

'I think I know,' said Virginia. 'I'd better go and tell him.'

At dawn the men from the ministry had put a token wire and post fencing round the throne. The ground was almost too hard to drive in the stakes and, in any case, the pilgrims had simply waited for them to retire and removed it. That morning, a doctor called to a woman giving birth in one of the caravans, had been startled by the organisation of the camp. From a distance, it appeared disordered, but he could see now why it had not been so easily dispersed. Every hundred yards there was a chemical toilet in a tent. From one of the larger caravans, tea was being served and there was a smell of breakfast cooking. Above all, everyone seemed cheerful, as if simply coming here had made them happy. They stood, blankets over their shoulders, faces turned to the sun, and smiled.

The Virgin, unseen, had attended the birth. On such occasions she found herself wishing that she had the powers of intercession credited to her by the Catholic Church. It was laid down, she knew, that since her first sin Eve must bring forth in pain but she couldn't help feeling that, by now, that grudge might be forgotten. Although she would not have dreamed of mentioning it, Mary had lately become interested in the feminist movement. It seemed to her that they had a great deal of justice and common sense on their side.

She told Humble that she had moved among the pilgrims and what she had seen. So many. The old and the young. The crippled, in particular, had affected her. She lowered her voice.

'To tell you the truth I wonder often why He permits so much affliction. He created such a beautiful earth. From the whole of your universe, this was the only blessed planet.' She sighed. 'I think He got bored. He washed His hands of it. That is the only possible explanation.'

The television people had caught up with the fact that something was going on. The only problem was the interference from the hum, that made commentary almost impossible. Hum said the stone and the people answered.

Watching from behind the recording van, Sandy saw the crowd part. Oliver came first with Dora behind him. Then Kitty, with her hand in Ralph's arm, and Virginia. Could that stumpy little figure be Humble, in the boots?

At the top of Poet's Walk, Oliver—apparently

oblivious of the pressing pilgrims—took his seat on the lap of the throne, looking out on a steel-cold sea. The orange winter mid-day sun stood still in the sky.

'Well, old flea, are you there? *Hic incipit vita*, eh? Is this where life begins? Again?'

There was no miracle, no healing grace, no chariot in the sky, no finger of God or any other power. Still, there were those who said that as Oliver stepped to the edge of the cliff and his soul departed his body, it could be seen leaping out as his earthly form fell. On television you could make it out quite clearly and you could hear the moment when the hum ceased and the pilgrims' song became a sigh.

13

Virginia went home. Ralph loved Kitty in St Marie-la-Douce and the dog Jackie and the cat Minette reached an accommodation. Alcestis disappeared, though so intense a presence is probably around somewhere, looking for trouble.

Humble took up travel. On Sir Oliver's small fortune, she was no longer obliged to go *ex corpore* but could enjoy a nice coach tour to the Italian Dolomites. Anywhere she arrived, this stolid, slightly forbidding traveller in the black laced shoes would make her way at once to the nearest church and ask for the Lady Chapel.

At Midsummer Sandy and Dora lay in their sleeping-bag on the leeward side of the stone. Sandy nuzzled the modest mound of her pregnancy.

'I can hear it!'

'That's the sausages. But you can feel him move. There! There's a flutter.'

'I was terrified you were going to jump as well, you know.'

'He wouldn't let me.'

'Nnn. I'll have to undo the zip. Move over.' Kneeling above her, a hand each side of her moonlit flesh, Sandy looked up and saw a shooting star. Or it might have been a satellite. Or a comet.

As he plunged into his proper home, above the shush of the sea there was a sound: a crack of laughter from the universe.